"Immedia[te] Housekeeper/nanny needed for two small children."

Paris rattled off the phone number, then looked up. "That's you, right?"

Mac could only nod. "But that ad just appeared in the paper this morning...."

"Oh, good, then I *am* the first." She seemed quite pleased with the notion. "Where are the children?"

"In the kitchen," he mumbled, disgruntled. "Eating breakfast." He considered telling her to leave and come back when he was ready to see her, but if she'd been into town, she already knew he was desperate.

"Oh," she said. With an apologetic grimace, her eyes flickered to her watch. "I guess it *is* early. I wasn't sure if you'd hired anyone else yet and if you hadn't, I wanted to be the first today."

"Believe me, you are," he grumbled. "But since you're here, you might as well come in."

Dear Reader,

Back by popular request is our deliciously delightful series—
BABY BOOM. We've asked some of your favorite authors in
Harlequin Romance® to bring you a few more special
deliveries—of the baby kind!

BABY BOOM is all about the true labor of love—parenthood
and how to survive it! And Patricia Knoll's *Project: Daddy*
brings you a man who didn't expect to be a dad just yet—
and a woman with enough love to help him make a family.

BABY BOOM

**When two's company and three (or four...or five)
is a family!**

PROJECT: DADDY

Patricia Knoll

HARLEQUIN®

TORONTO • NEW YORK • LONDON
AMSTERDAM • PARIS • SYDNEY • HAMBURG
STOCKHOLM • ATHENS • TOKYO • MILAN • MADRID
PRAGUE • WARSAW • BUDAPEST • AUCKLAND

To Barbara McMahon and Renee Roszel,
whom I love for their writing and for their friendship.

ISBN 0-373-03610-8

PROJECT: DADDY

First North American Publication 2000.

Copyright © 2000 by Patricia Knoll.

This edition published by arrangement with Harlequin Books S.A.

® and TM are trademarks of the publisher. Trademarks indicated with
® are registered in the United States Patent and Trademark Office, the
Canadian Trade Marks Office and in other countries.

Visit us at www.eHarlequin.com

Printed in U.S.A.

CHAPTER ONE

MACKENZIE—Mac—Weston felt as if he'd been picked up by a whirlwind—a five-and-a-half-foot tall one with curly strawberry-blond hair and big green eyes. A whirlwind with the unlikely name of Paris Katharine Barbour who had snatched him up at eight o'clock that morning and danced him merrily from one end of Cliff County to the other.

He'd spent half an hour standing in this very spot trying to figure out exactly how it had happened. He hooked his hands into the back pockets of his jeans and stared out at the darkness, then grunted in frustration when he felt the loose jeans begin to slide down his hips. He stuck his thumbs through the belt loops and jerked them back up again. He should have put on a belt. All his jeans were loose these days, had been for months, but he hadn't cared enough to do more than tighten his belt another notch and keep wearing them. He didn't want new ones, couldn't afford them. Anyway, he'd be horsewhipped before he'd go into Cliffside to buy them.

His jeans weren't his immediate problem, though. Ms. Paris Katharine was a more urgent dilemma right now.

Mac thought back carefully over the conversation he'd had with her when she'd arrived at his door, suitcase in hand and bright smile on face.

He rubbed his jaw, unshaven for two days, and tried to pinpoint exactly where the whole situation had begun to go south on him....

5

"Mr. Weston?" she asked, sidling through the front door as soon as he'd opened it. She grinned up at him, dazzling him with a set of beautiful white teeth and a bow-shaped smile. "I'm Paris Barbour. The new housekeeper and nanny." She peeked past his shoulder. "Why don't I just come right in?"

"The new...?" Staggered by the full wattage of that smile, he stood with the door open, gaping at her as her long skirt, brightly patterned in shades of red, purple and yellow, swirled through the door behind her.

Paris reached back, gently pried the door from his grip and shut it firmly as if to assert that she was in now and wouldn't be dislodged. Flashing him a supremely confident look, she set down her suitcase and her purse with a finality that had his stunned eyes narrowing suspiciously.

"Paris...?"

"Barbour," she supplied, her gaze darting around the foyer, taking in the putty-colored native stone beneath their feet and the pale yellow walls. "Paris Katharine Barbour. Fancy name, but one of my mom's favorite movies was *Summertime* with Katharine Hepburn and Rossano Brazzi. The movie takes place in Venice, so Mom wanted to name me Venice Katharine—I think she identified with the idea of an older woman having a fling because she never really did anything outrageous in her life, my mom I mean, but my dad put his foot down and said he'd waited fifty years to have a child and no daughter of his was going to have such an unfeminine name, so they called me Paris instead." She shrugged, then dazzled him with that smile once again. "I guess that's okay. It's better than being called Zurich or Detroit, wouldn't you say?"

Mac couldn't say anything. He was drowning in her

torrent of words. It took him a few seconds to gasp his way to the surface. If he hadn't witnessed it, he never would have believed a person could pack so many words into a single breath. Finally, he said, "Wha...why did you say you're here?"

"Your advertisement, remember? I'm answering it."

"In *person?*"

His appalled question caused a moment of doubt to flash in her eyes but it was quickly hidden by bravado. She lifted a delicately square chin and said, "Yes. Your ad sounded quite urgent, so I thought it would be best if I started work right away." She reached into her pocket, pulled out a newspaper clipping and held it up. "Immediate position available," she read. "Housekeeper/nanny needed for two small children. Competitive salary and benefits offered." She rattled off the phone number then looked up. "That's you, right?"

Mac could only nod, still taken aback by her pushiness. "But that ad just appeared in the paper this morning...."

"Oh, good, then I *am* the first." She seemed quite pleased with the notion.

"How'd you find me? I only gave the number."

She waved airily. "Oh, that doesn't matter, does it? I'm here now and that's what's important." She rubbed her palms together expectantly and turned her head from side to side, peeking past his shoulder. That incredible hair of hers shifted softly, catching the weak morning light and magnifying its power. "Where are the children?"

Mac pushed his own too-long, damp hair out of his eyes and pulled the front of his shirt together—she'd caught him fresh out of the shower—and began to do up the buttons as he observed her and tried to get his brain to work even though it hadn't yet been jump-started with a dose of caffeine. She made him think of that kids' movie about the nanny who had blown in on the wind. *Mary Poppins,* that was the name. Maybe he'd better check outside and see if a gale had kicked up when he wasn't looking.

"In the kitchen," he mumbled, disgruntled. "Eating breakfast." He considered telling her to leave and come back when he was ready to see her, but if she'd been into Cliffside, she already knew he was desperate for someone to watch Elly and Simon. No doubt, she also knew a great many other things about him, which made him wonder why she'd come here at all. On the other hand, she'd been in such a hurry, she might not have stopped in town.

"Oh," she said. With an apologetic grimace, her eyes flickered to her watch. "I guess it *is* early. I wasn't sure if you'd hired anyone else yet and if you hadn't, I wanted to be the first one here today."

"Believe me, you are," he grumbled. "Since you're here, you might as well come on into the kitchen." He led the way up the short flight of steps from the entryway to the living room, and his gaze darted around self-consciously. It hadn't bothered him before to let people see the place, bare and uninviting as it was, but something about this bright-eyed woman made him glance back for her reaction. It was a mistake. Her burnished hair and swirling skirt made it look as though someone had trapped a butterfly in the icy gray-and-whiteness of his living room.

Surprisingly, she didn't say anything about the bareness of the room. After a moment, he wondered if she'd even noticed it because her gaze was fixed on the huge plate glass windows.

"Incredible view," she murmured, evidently in awe of the vast expanse of ocean visible beyond the glass. The water was capped by flecks of white foam thrown up by the breeze and brightened by the morning sun slanting in from the east. "I've always wanted to live near the ocean."

He'd heard that line before. Annoyed, he said, "If that's your only reason for wanting this job, you're in the wrong place."

She turned swiftly and gave him a direct look from those clear green eyes. "It's not my only reason. In fact, it's not a reason at all. I didn't know about the ocean view, remember? I'm here because I need a job and this is one I'll be good at."

Mac gave her the full force of his frown, the one he'd been told made him look like a grizzly bear with indigestion. The butterfly didn't back down from the impact of it, but tilted her head and gave him another of those expectant looks as if she was asking if he had any other comments to make.

He did. "Well, we'll see about that. Come on." Turning, he led the way past the windows, through the formal dining room which held nothing but a built-in sideboard, empty of all but a gray film of dust, and through a wide archway into the kitchen.

He heard her rock to a stop behind him and looked back to see her taking in the sight of the kitchen. It was certainly impressive. On the right, a stainless steel restaurant-quality range and oven stood beside a glass-fronted refrigerator. On the left were a double sink, a vegetable sink, and long, bare white-tiled counters. All the cabinet fronts were painted stark white and had plain steel hardware. A food preparation island in the middle of the room was topped by a concrete slab that he'd been assured was the height of home fashion.

"When does the surgical team arrive?" Paris murmured, then gave him an apologetic look and clamped her lips shut.

He frowned at her again, although he agreed with her assessment. However, he hadn't been the one to choose the decor, and it didn't really matter to him. It was a kitchen, he could get food there, after a fashion, and that's all that mattered, or had been all that mattered until a few days ago. Now he spent more time there and the desolate place was beginning to get on his nerves.

He gestured for her to follow him to a bay window. In the alcove was a chrome and red vinyl dinette set straight out of the nineteen fifties. It was a castoff from his parents' house and the only thing in the place with a speck of personality. Paris must have thought so, too, because her gaze swept over it appreciatively before landing on his niece and nephew.

Four-year-old Elly knelt on one of the chairs where he had settled her before he and Simon had headed for the shower. She was rocking rhythmically as she leaned over the table and ate from a bowl. Her head full of coppery curls had gone uncombed since she'd arrived at Uncle Mac's house. Eighteen-month-old Simon, also a curly redhead, was perched on a stack of books and tied securely onto the chair with a necktie that ran beneath his armpits and was knotted behind him. Both children looked up when the adults entered. Their faces were smeared with chocolate, giving them a comical appearance, but neither child smiled. Reacting to the sight of yet another stranger, Elly scooted down from her chair and hurried around to stand protectively beside her baby brother.

It made Mac uncomfortable to meet the solemn blue eyes of his niece and nephew, but he didn't know quite how to remedy the problem. He'd rarely seen them before their arrival two days ago and he knew absolutely nothing about kids, could barely even remember his own childhood, in fact.

Paris flashed one of her vivid smiles at the two kids who blinked at her hesitantly. "Hello," she said. "My name is Paris. What's yours?"

Elly gave Mac a questioning glance and he nodded reassuringly even as he wondered at this about-face. Two days ago, the little girl had been afraid of *him*. Now she was looking to him for reassurance. Finally, Elly lifted a chocolate-covered hand to point to herself. "Elly," she said. "And that's Simon. He's just a baby."

"So I see." Paris moved toward the table and glanced into the children's bowls. Mac shuffled his feet and looked down when he saw the amazement that crossed her face. "What are you having for breakfast?" she asked in a strangled voice.

"Choc'late bars," Elly answered, returning to her own bowl and scooping up another fingerful. "It's good."

Mac felt Paris's gaze on him and he met it with a one-shouldered shrug. "Haven't had time to get to the grocery store," he muttered, then could have kicked himself for offering an explanation to this woman he didn't even know.

She brightened and he figured she was probably laughing at him. "Then that's something I can handle for you, isn't it?" Seeing that Elly was finished with her breakfast, Paris flashed a quick look around the untarnished kitchen and said, "Why don't we wash your hands before you get down?"

Before Elly could answer, Paris tore paper towels from a roll by the sink, wet them and began wiping Elly's hands free of chocolate. Elly gave Paris a startled look as if she wanted to pull away, but Paris began prattling on about what a beautiful day it was and how lucky they were to live by the ocean, and had they seen the seagulls flying overhead that morning? In the face of such good-natured chatter, cautious Elly relaxed. She even offered Paris a tiny, tentative smile.

Mac felt disgruntled. Elly hadn't allowed him to touch her until late last night, screaming for her mother each time he tried to do something for her. Poor kid, her mother was long gone. Simon, on the other hand, seemed to like Mac. At least he didn't holler whenever Mac came near him.

Just so she wouldn't think he was completely hopeless, Mac got both children glasses of water to drink, but when she treated him to another of those questioning looks he had to admit, "No milk, either."

He hustled the children into the family room to watch Saturday morning cartoons. When they were lying on the floor in front of the screen, he breathed a sigh of relief that they'd be safely occupied for a while, and turned back to the kitchen. He'd never interviewed a housekeeper/nanny before, but he had a basic idea of what questions he needed to ask. Any good parent, even a temporary one, knew that there were certain things kids needed: food, cleanliness, companionship, discipline. He figured if he paid for the first one, and paid the nanny enough, she could provide the rest of the list.

In the kitchen, he found that Paris was busy going through the cupboards and refrigerator. She had located a piece of paper and a pencil and was making a list.

"Wait," he said, holding up his hand. "Before you

make plans to move in and take over, I need to know a few things about you.''

"Sure," she answered breezily, as she clucked over the bareness of his refrigerator. He frowned at her. It wasn't bare. He had two six-packs of beer and a couple of stale doughnuts in there, as well as five different kinds of gourmet mustard. He didn't usually eat at home, but picked up breakfast, lunch and dinner at any fast-food place he happened to pass on his way to and from work.

"My name is Paris...oh, I already told you my name. I'm a widow." He couldn't read her expression or her tone of voice when she said that, but he thought she sounded very matter-of-fact. "I need a job and this looks like something I can do."

Mac strolled over to where she was standing, slapped his hand against the refrigerator door to shut it, and said, "What exactly do you mean by that?"

She tilted her head and smiled. A California jay had nothing on this girl in the perkiness department. "It means I can take care of this house and your children."

"They're not my children," he admitted, then stepped back when he realized he could detect the scent of her perfume. It smelled like April violets and somehow went straight to his head. He needed coffee. Turning away, he reached for the coffeemaker and began making the brew.

"They're not?"

"Elly and Simon are my sister's kids. Sheila arrived a couple of days ago, just after I got home from work and said she needed for me to take care of them for a while. She was on her way to Africa on a photographic safari."

"She's a photographer?"

Mac growled, "She doesn't know a lens cap from a viewfinder. Her new boyfriend is a photographer and she went along to keep him company. Unfortunately, she had two little responsibilities standing in her way.'' As Paris made a soft sound of distress, Mac viciously ripped the plastic lid off a can of coffee and scooped grounds into the filter. It still infuriated him that Sheila had shown up blithely assuming that he would take the kids, kissed them goodbye and left them, wailing loudly, in his faulty care.

He didn't know why he was surprised. The whole family had spoiled Sheila and done her bidding throughout her life. Her divorce had come about because her husband, as feckless and selfish as she, wouldn't cater to her the way the Weston family had. The husband had taken off shortly after the divorce, had never even seen Simon. When Sheila had decided to go on safari, big brother Mac had seemed the logical choice to take care of her children.

Poor little tykes, he thought, pouring water into the coffeemaker and switching it on. Dragged from pillar to post their whole lives, then left in the care of the one person who was the least likely to know what to do with them. Surreptitiously, he studied Paris who had seated herself at the table after carefully checking to make sure she'd cleaned up all chocolate smears. He wondered how capable she was of caring for the two children. So far, he hadn't pulled any hard information out of her except that she was a widow. His gaze drifted over her as he wondered what had become of her husband and how long the man had been dead. She didn't seem too broken up, but then, who was he to judge how misfortune affected anyone? The good citizens of Cliffside said the lousy things that had happened in his life had only served to make him meaner and more stubborn. Too bad he couldn't disagree with them.

He poured coffee for both of them and handed her a cup. She sipped it cautiously and opened her mouth as if to ask for cream or milk, then apparently recalled that he had none, so she drank stoically. Mac supposed he shouldn't have made it the way he usually did, strong enough to float an ax handle.

"Do you have a resume?" he asked abruptly.

"Certainly." She had left her suitcase by the front door, but had set her purse on one of the kitchen chairs while tending to Elly. Paris opened the large bag and pulled out an envelope which she handed to him with a flourish, her eyes full of the same bravado he'd seen moments before. Mac wondered about that as he pulled out the folded page and smoothed it.

He scanned it quickly and his eyebrows inched up. Finally, he bent down one corner of the paper and looked at her over the top. She seemed to be busy examining the blue sky outside the window. When she felt him looking at her, she brought her attention back to him and gave him a sprightly smile. "Impressive, isn't it?" she asked on a hopeful note.

Mac stared at her, stared at the paper, then at her again. "Organized the annual fund-raiser for the Junior League?"

"And topped our previous year's earnings, I might add," she said with a firm nod and a tap of her fingernail on the tabletop.

"Chairman of the country club ball committee?"

"Everyone in attendance said it was the best ball they'd ever seen."

"Scandinavian cooking classes?"

"My Danish *frikadellar* are to die for," she assured him as she linked her fingers together loosely on the tabletop and sat forward as if waiting for his applause.

He scanned the resume again, just in case he'd missed something. "There's no evidence here that you've ever held a real, salary-paying job."

Her hands tightened around each other. "Oh?"

"Have you?" he prompted.

"Held a salaried position? Noooo," she answered, drawing the word out. "I can't say that I have."

"All you've ever done is volunteer work?"

"I've done it very well, though."

"Mrs. Barbour..."

"Paris, please."

He ignored her interruption and soldiered on. "These accomplishments have nothing to do with taking care of children or running a house."

"That's not true. If you'll look carefully, you'll see I had extensive experience doing baby-sitting all through high school. I didn't get an allowance so that was how I earned spending money. Also, I spent a summer caring for two children while their mom was sick."

He lifted a skeptical eyebrow. "Baby-sitting is far different than being a nanny."

"The duties are basically the same."

"But the responsibility isn't. Taking care of two children for a few hours is very different than caring for them day in and day out."

"That's true," she agreed. "Fortunately, I'm versatile and can learn quickly. Why, I'd never even been involved with a fund-raiser before I headed up the one for the Junior League, but it did far better than expected."

Mac's eyes narrowed. "That's fine, but when exactly was the last time you actually took care of children?"

Her eyes made a quick survey of the corners of the room as if looking for spider webs—like the ones she was catching herself in, Mac thought cynically. "About six years ago," she admitted in a rush, giving him a sincere nod that set her hair to bouncing around her shoulders. "However, it's a skill I've never forgotten, and truly, I can do anything I set my mind to. Like I said, I'm a quick learner."

And a fast talker, he thought, trying to suppress the admiration he felt for her determination. "Have you ever run a house?"

"Of course," she answered firmly, but her eyes couldn't quite meet his. "Well, I supervised."

With a last disparaging glance at her resume, Mac refolded it and shoved it back into the envelope. He didn't know what kind of game she was playing, but he wanted no part of it. "Why would a society girl like you want this job?"

"I'm *not* a society girl. At least, not any longer. I need to provide for myself. This is a job that I can do. You won't be taking any risk by hiring me," she went on fervently. "There are character references on my resume who will vouch for my honesty. I'm a good cook, anybody can clean house, and what I don't know about taking care of children, I can learn."

"No," he began, shaking his head, but she cut him off.

"A two-week trial, then," she pleaded, her eyes going deep green in her distress. "That's all I ask."

Mac felt an uncomfortable stillness within him as he looked at the need in her eyes. He wanted to back away like a crab scrambling across the sand. Wasn't it enough that he had these two kids to look out for? He didn't want anyone else around who had needs of any kind that he would deal with. Before he could react, she reached across the table and cupped her hand over his, squeezing firmly as she tried to convince him.

Mac reacted as if a live wire had wrapped itself around his wrist. He recoiled and she snatched her hand away. She flushed, obviously embarrassed by what she'd done and stunned by his reaction. Shifting in his chair, he sat back and tried to cover his retreat with a sip of coffee.

What the heck had that been about? he wondered. No mystery, he decided after a moment. He'd gone too long without having a woman around and it just proved he didn't need this one around, either.

Mac cleared his throat. "I'm sorry, but you won't do, Mrs. Barbour. I need someone with more experience."

"But I'm reliable," she said, desperately. Pointing toward the room where the children were watching cartoons, she said, "You could see for yourself that Elly liked me. That's something I can build on. Besides," she went on in a breathless tone, as if she'd used up all her ammunition and was prepared to go down fighting anyway, "The economy is good right now, there are all kinds of jobs available for anyone who wants one—"

"Then why don't you try for one of those?" Mac broke in.

Her mouth opened and closed. He had her there and it took her a moment to regroup and come charging back.

"I would prefer to work in a home. I was trying to say that it's possible you might have trouble finding someone who'd like to work out here. It's somewhat…isolated."

The words *desolate* and *godforsaken*, spoken in the voice of his ex-fiancée, Judith, echoed in his mind. She'd wanted to live near the ocean but only if there were plenty of socializing opportunities, preferably a yacht club nearby. She hadn't been too thrilled with his plan to build the house near his hometown of Cliffside on this rocky section of coast. He'd partially redeemed himself in her eyes by letting her take over the interior design of the place—which was how he'd ended up living in something that looked like the guts of an iceberg.

He couldn't imagine that Miss Country Club Ball would turn out to be any different than Judith. On the other hand, he was afraid this girl had a point. No one from Cliffside would want to work for him and he had only today and tomorrow to find someone to care for Elly and Simon. He had to be at work on Monday or risk losing his own job. He had a bad feeling about this, though. A really bad feeling. This girl was too attractive, too alive to be around him, around this place that was full of raw emotions and bad memories. No doubt it was unhealthy for Elly and Simon, too, but they were stuck with it.

But Elly and Simon were the ones he had to consider, not himself. He might resent Sheila for dumping them on him, but he had to do his best by them. Despite what the locals might think, he always fulfilled his responsibilities.

He couldn't have her here, though. He stared at Paris's hopeful, earnest face for several seconds and was opening his mouth to say once more that she wouldn't do when Simon came into the room. He was dragging his blanket and carrying a book under his arm.

"Wead," Simon grunted, holding up the book.

Relieved because he could use the little boy as an excuse to end this interview and send Paris on her way, Mac reached for his nephew. Simon ignored Mac's outstretched hand, skirted around him, and headed straight for Paris who looked startled, but pulled the baby into her lap and examined the book.

"Animals," she said. "My favorite subject."

Satisfied, Simon leaned back against her, popped his thumb into his mouth, and reached up to begin twirling a lock of her hair around his finger. Once again, Paris looked surprised, but she didn't pull away, earning herself points with both Simon and Mac.

As she opened the book and began reading about Simon's favorite animals, Mac felt himself soften toward her. Maybe it was true that kids and dogs were good judges of who to trust. If so, Simon obviously trusted Paris.

Still, she had little experience or training. A woman from the country club set had no business here, and why would she want the job, anyway? He wasn't satisfied with her explanation, what there was of it, and wanted more answers, but getting more answers would mean keeping her around and it was best if he hustled her out the door as quickly as possible. And he would, too, as soon as she finished reading to Simon.

As he watched, Paris snuggled Simon close and turned so the sunlight that had sneaked in the window could fall on the book. It fell on her hair, as well, burnishing it gold, and giving her skin a luminous clarity. To his horror, Mac felt as if that light was reaching toward him. Mentally, he backed away, fabricating imaginary barriers as he went, but when Simon looked up unexpectedly and gave his uncle a grin for the first time since his arrival, Mac felt something inside himself crumple and give way. Although it was the last thing he would have expected to come out of his mouth, he abruptly said, "Two weeks."

Paris placed her finger on the page and glanced up curiously. "Excuse me?"

Feeling like five kinds of a fool, Mac said, "You can

have a two-week trial. Then we'll see. And I should warn you that I don't know how long the job will last. Sheila could return next week or next year, but I suspect she'll be gone for a while. We'll start with two weeks.''

Relief and joy flooded her face, brightening her eyes. "You won't regret it, Mr. Weston."

He already did. Then to make sure she knew he was boss, he repeated it. "Two-week trial. That's all. If it doesn't work out, we'll end it right there, no hard feelings on either side."

She smiled as if he'd handed her a gift. All her other smiles had been designed to charm him and get what she wanted. He was used to that kind. This one was pure pleasure and gratitude as if he'd done a great thing and was a heck of a nice guy.

Mac couldn't remember the last time someone had looked at him like that, if anyone ever had. Again, he felt that odd softening going on in his gut and he scowled to fight it off.

"Two weeks," Paris said, obviously trying to hide her glee and appear professional. "That sounds perfectly fair." She gave Simon a hug. "Why don't I get started as soon as I finish this book?"

CHAPTER TWO

AND get started she had. She had taken the money he'd given her and started out to stock up the pantry. He'd headed her off before she left.

"Go into Alban. It's fifteen miles down the highway."

Paris, busy double-checking her shopping list, looked up in surprise. "I can go to Cliffside. It's much closer."

"And prices are higher. Go to Alban. There's a supermarket there."

She started to protest again, but he held up his hand. "While you're gone, I'll check your references."

Her expression told him she wanted to argue, but she kept a lid on it. He hadn't meant to make it sound like coercion, but if it would get her to do as he asked without having to go into detailed explanations, he would let her think what she liked.

Finally, her lips pinched together and she nodded. "All right."

He could tell she was put out, though he wasn't sure if it was directed at him for being so insistent, or herself for giving in so easily. He saw a small war waging in her as if she was battling to keep her thoughts to herself. He had to admire that, but he didn't want to because it would make her too real to him, too much a person.

He'd known her less than an hour, and he didn't intend to get to know her much better. After all, she was an employee and he'd learned the hard way that employer/employee familiarity was to be avoided at all costs. In spite of that resolution, he found himself offering the use of his truck for her trip to Alban.

"Is that it?" she asked, nodding toward the ten-year-old battle-scarred extended cab pickup truck parked in the driveway.

"Yes. You'll need space for all the items on that list."

The annoyance he'd seen in her eyes was replaced by amusement. "No thanks. I don't like driving unfamiliar vehicles. I'll take my own car." She hesitated, then pushed her unruly hair back from her face and met his gaze. "I just brought in one suitcase. Since I'm going to be staying, I might as well bring in everything to make room for the groceries in my car."

With that, she whirled out the door and left him to trail along in her wake battling his own irritation that she'd turned the tables on him. Still, he felt another spurt of grudging admiration at the way she'd done it.

They unloaded her car and he carried everything inside while she'd roared away in the small compact that sounded as if it badly needed a tune-up. As he placed her things in the room she'd chosen next to the children's then went to check on Elly and Simon, Mac speculated that, given her resume, she'd probably been accustomed to a better car but she'd obviously fallen on hard times. Or hard times had fallen on her.

That made two of them. He'd had a fancy, fully-loaded sport utility vehicle that had impressed the heck out of the neighborhood, as well as a midnight-blue sports car that had been his pride, but he'd sold them both without a qualm when he'd needed money. Funny how little either of those had mattered when weighed against his good name.

Now as he stared out at the ocean, Mac, who hadn't been curious about much of anything for more than a year now, wondered what she'd given up, and why, to be where she was now—a nanny and housekeeper to a lonely man and two abandoned kids.

Paris quietly pulled the bedroom door almost closed behind her, leaving it open just enough to provide a night light for the children and enable her to hear them if they cried out. After peeking down the long, bare hall to make sure she was alone, she allowed her shoulders to slump wearily as she headed for her own room next door.

She was grateful that Elly and Simon had been tired enough to go right to sleep. Though she didn't know very much about children, she fully understood what it was like to have the world turn upside down and land on top of her and that's exactly what Elly and Simon had experienced. She'd known them less than fourteen hours, but she wanted to try and make things easier for them. It broke her heart to see sturdy little Elly's stoic acceptance of her circumstances and her protectiveness toward Simon. Elly had warmed toward Paris during the course of the day and they had made a cautious start toward being friends. When Simon had lost some of his shyness and begun to talk to Paris, Elly had interpreted his baby talk. Still, Paris wondered if the little girl would call out in the night if she was frightened. Hoping she would, and that Paris herself would waken if she was needed, she turned her thoughts to her own situation.

Sheer nerve and desperation had carried her through the day and she was bone-tired. Rubbing her knuckles across her forehead, she sank onto the side of the bed and asked herself what in the world she'd gotten into.

The newspaper ad had seemed like a wonderful gift when she'd first seen it; work she knew she could do in an out-of-the way place where no one knew or cared about her, but this…

Dismayed, she looked around at the stark place. A bed, a table, and a lamp were the entire furnishings, the bleakness of it almost identical to the children's room which held only a baby playpen and a single bed. Every item looked as though it had been recently purchased at a rummage sale. Elly's bed still had a little yellow stick-on tag with the price printed by hand. Paris wondered if Mac had run out to scavenge whatever he could as soon as he knew he had to keep the children. She admired that, even as she knew he probably only saw it as doing his duty.

The saddest thing she'd seen among the children's belongings, though, was the lack of toys and clothes in the closet, as if their mother couldn't be bothered to bring all they might need or want. She'd wanted to cry at the sight. Her horror at the way they'd been abandoned had been matched by her distress over their uncle's ineptitude. Truthfully though, she couldn't say he didn't care about them. Mac, at least, had some sense of responsibility, certainly more than his sister had.

The sight of the imposing glass-and-cedar home had given her pause when she had first sighted it that morning, but it was so beautiful, and so perfectly positioned on the cliff overlooking the Pacific, she had decided to at least ask about the job. The closer she'd come to the door, the more she had tightened up on her courage until even the sight of the imposing man who answered it couldn't stop her from barreling inside as if she had every right to be there.

She knew she had given Mac an erroneous impression of herself, maybe even a wrong one, letting him think she was bold and outspoken, when in truth, she was outgoing but not bossy. Usually, only nervousness made her that way. When she had left her small hometown of Hadley in the Imperial Valley, though, she had decided that she had to change. Her days of depending on others to look out for her were over. Being dependent had gained her nothing but a mountain of debts and a broken heart.

Shuddering at the memory of her flight from Hadley, and some of the things that had happened since, she stood suddenly and began unpacking her suitcase, laying the items she would need for the night on the bed and making a mental note to find boxes of some kind to use as a makeshift dresser.

She was wildly curious to know why the house was so bare. Couldn't he afford furniture? Didn't he want any? As yet, she didn't know him well enough to judge whether or not he seemed content with so little, but somehow she didn't think it mattered to him.

Paris considered the man who had hired her. Mac seemed tense, watchful. More than once that day she'd felt his attention on her and looked up to find him viewing her with a gaze that seemed to be questioning her actions and motives. Not that she blamed him. She knew her resume was far less than impressive—as were her references. However, what Mac had learned about her must have been satisfactory because he hadn't backed down on his offer to hire her.

Although she was grateful for the job, she wondered why she'd been awarded it. She wasn't going to ask him and risk being told it was all a terrible mistake and she'd have to go.

"Avoidance at all costs," she murmured to herself, wincing guiltily as she acknowledged it was a character flaw she was trying to overcome. She wouldn't be in this predicament now if she hadn't been so intent on pretending that everything was okay with Keith, if she hadn't avoided knowing that he was gullibly squandering his own fortune and everything she'd inherited from her parents, if she hadn't helped him squander it until she'd finally wised up.

Shaking off those maudlin thoughts, Paris moved her tired body out of the room and into the hallway to speak to her new boss. When she got no answer to her knock on his bedroom door, she knew she'd have to search the house for him. "Shouldn't be hard to find," she whispered to herself, examining the picture-free walls and pristine carpet. "He can't exactly hide behind the furniture."

Telling herself that she *wasn't* intimidated by this brooding, disturbing man, Paris walked briskly through the house until she found him before the huge plate glass of the living room windows, staring out into the night. She stopped and hung back so that her reflection wouldn't catch his attention.

Mac stood with his head thrust forward, causing his midnight-black hair to fall over his forehead. His hands were thrust into the back pockets of his jeans. Though he was physically fit and his arms were roped with muscles, he was too skinny. His clothes hung on a frame that seemed to carry twenty pounds less than it should. She doubted that he had thinned down on purpose. He had told her he was a carpenter and she knew he needed strength and stamina for such a job. Another quick examination of the living room had her wondering if he was more than a carpenter. He may have built this place himself, and she had a hunch he'd also had a hand in designing it. Something about the design of the house, the high ceilings and view of the ocean made her picture him bending over a draftsman's table, carefully laying out the plans.

His face was thin and gaunt, as well, his dark eyes shadowed, hiding secrets. He stood with one shoulder turned slightly toward the window in a way that made her think of someone shouldering a burden, taking on yet another heavy load. She had never considered herself to be particularly astute at reading people. If she had, she certainly would have tried to keep Keith from giving their money to fast-talking charlatans. She could read Mac Weston, though, and what she saw told her he had been through rough times and they still weren't behind him.

Against her will, she felt herself drawn to him as she was to his niece and nephew. She had no idea what his story was, but it struck a chord in her and made her more curious about him. Paris reminded herself that she needed to remember that this was just a job, one she would hold until she got back on her feet and decided what she was going to do with the rest of her life.

She must have moved or made a sound, because Mac's head came up and the brooding look in his eyes gave way to caution as if he feared he'd revealed something of himself. He had, but she pretended as if she hadn't seen it. "Is something wrong?" he asked. "The kids..."

"Are asleep," she said, forcing briskness into her voice and striding into the room. Strangely, she felt her exhaustion fall away and vitality take its place as she joined him. "I left their door open so I could hear them. Will they sleep all night?"

"They've only been here two nights, and they haven't slept much either night." Mac ran his hand over his face. Paris knew he hadn't either.

"I came to find out when you want breakfast." She hadn't been a housekeeper for very long, but she knew that was the kind of question she was supposed to ask. After all, her housekeeper used to ask her that question.

"Feed them whenever they get hungry," he answered, his dark eyes regarding her in some confusion.

"No, I mean you, what time do you want your breakfast?"

"I can take care of myself," he said gruffly, as if it didn't matter. "That's not why I hired you. You're here to take care of Elly and Simon."

Paris took exception to his dismissive tone. "And this house and everything connected with it, right? Including meals."

"You don't have to worry about me. I'll get my own food."

Even though she hadn't intended to, Paris glanced at the way his jeans hung on his frame. Against her will, her lips tilted into a smile as if to say he hadn't been doing such a good job of feeding himself. "You hired me to cook and that's what I intend to—"

"No," he said, scowling at her. "I don't need you fussing over me."

Her eyes widened. "Fussing? I'm trying to do my job."

"Which is to take care of Elly and Simon, not me."

Paris could only stare. What kind of man was this who couldn't accept anything from someone he'd *hired* to help him? A stubborn and proud one, she concluded.

"Wait a minute, Mr. Weston…"

Wincing, he held up his hand. "Mac, please," he said.

"Mac, then." She took a breath. "Although I admit I don't have much experience as a housekeeper…"

"Much?" he asked, his black brows rising skeptically.

"All right. Very little actual hands-on experience as a housekeeper," she said, exasperated. "But I've been around many of them and their job is to cook and care for the whole family, not just the children."

"Think of yourself as a pioneer in the housekeeping field, then Mrs. Barbour," he suggested.

"Paris." This time she was the one to do the correcting and was surprised to discover it felt good.

"You don't have to worry about me. Just take care of the kids so I can get to work and hang onto the job that provides for all of us."

Paris didn't much like the way he said that, as if what she did with the kids wasn't important as long as they were cared for. Maybe she had given him too much credit when considering how generous he was to take in Elly and Simon. It didn't sound as though he had any intention of being involved with them at all.

To test the waters, she asked, "And what time will you be coming home in the evenings? I'm sure you'll want to spend some quality time with the children when you do."

His head drew back. Was that panic she saw flash in his eyes? Puzzled, she blinked at him.

"I'll be home when I get home. This is the busy season in the construction industry and we work as many hours as we can before the winter rains hit. In fact, I often work weekends."

Dismayed, Paris couldn't think of a thing to say. She understood he had to work, but he sounded as if he wanted to do all he could to *avoid* coming home to Elly and Simon. At this point, she was tempted to back away, to accept what he said and meekly agree to it. She'd done that so often with Keith who'd had so many good-natured stories and excuses for his actions that she'd become mired in his logic. This was different, though. In her discussions with Keith, she'd had only herself to consider. Now she had to think about two children and what was best for them. Being stuck all day with the housekeeper/nanny, no matter how devoted, wasn't best for them. For their sake, she went on instead of backing off as she might have done before.

"So you're saying that we should just expect you when we see you?"

"That about covers it. I'm trusting you to take care of everything they need." His eyes narrowed. "I thought I'd made that clear this morning."

"I understand what my duties are, I just don't understand what you think yours are if not to be a caring, loving presence for them."

Annoyance swept over his face. She didn't need any kind of interpreter to tell her that she'd gone too far, but she couldn't back down even if she got fired as the culmination of her first day of work.

He stepped forward and leaned in to look into her eyes. Toughness and irritation seemed to vibrate from him like light waves. "If I get fired, I'll be a constant presence for them since I'll be hanging around the house all day, but I'd rather not get fired, if it's all the same to you."

Paris's lips thinned as she met his gaze. Because she couldn't trust herself to speak, she nodded once, quickly and he answered with a nod of his own as if they'd sealed a bargain.

Mac started to step away, then checked himself as if he had more to say. Her eyes holding his, Paris waited for what else would come. He opened his mouth, then paused. His gaze drifted from hers, then dropped lower, touching on her cheek, then her lips. She felt a tingling there which seemed to sweep down her throat and chest to strike with a thud in the center of her stomach. Jerking in a huge breath, she stepped back.

He blinked as if a fingersnap had roused him, and he, too, stepped back. Mac cleared his throat, stuck his hands, palm out into the back pockets of his jeans, then pulled them out again. "I called your references."

"And?" Paris couldn't help the caution in her voice.

"They checked out, even though that girl you had listed, Carolyn, said she hadn't seen you in five years."

Paris's hands drifted up to play with the collar of her blouse. "Has it been that long?"

"And the man—your family doctor? Well, he could barely stop laughing long enough for me to ask the questions, but he did confirm the excellent state of your health."

"Laughing?"

"Apparently, he thought the idea of you being a housekeeper and nanny was pretty funny."

"Well," Paris said primly. "Dr. Gaddis is…easily amused."

"Mm-hm."

He obviously didn't believe that stretching of the truth, so she dropped it and said, "The important thing is that they could vouch for my character, right? So my two-week trial is on?"

"Looks like." Mac tilted his head and gave her a speculative look as if once again, there was more he wanted to say. Instead, he turned abruptly and started from the room. "I'm going to bed. Wake me if you need help with the kids in the night."

Paris stared at his disappearing back. "Well, I'll be

darned,'' she murmured. In one breath he'd virtually turned the kids and their complete care over to her, and in the next, he'd subtly reminded her that he was watching her closely.

It wasn't fair, she thought grumpily, as she switched off the living room light and made her way to her own room. She wanted to slot him into a neat pigeonhole in her mind, but he wouldn't fit.

Her father had been a robust, yet simple man whose life had revolved around planting and harvesting, watching the weather and gauging how many cubic feet of water he would need for irrigating his celery crop. Her husband Keith had been sweet and shy, eager to please absolutely everyone around him.

This man had more facets than a fistful of diamonds. She frowned at that poor analogy. There was nothing precious or jewel-like about him, though he certainly seemed to have the hardness of a diamond. Bemused, she prepared for bed.

Paris woke up when a small hand pinched her nostrils shut. Gasping, she jerked into wakefulness and reached out to grab Elly's wrist and pull it away.

"You 'wake?" the little girl whispered, putting her face up close to Paris's.

"I am now," Paris admitted, struggling upward. She reached out to snap on the light.

In the sudden brightness, she and Elly blinked at each other. The little girl's fiery curls tumbled about her face, her eyes were full of tears and her bottom lip trembled. She clutched a tattered stuffed rabbit to her chest and was holding one of its ears to her cheek.

"Simon wants to sleep with you," she announced.

"He's scared and he wants to get in your bed. He wants me to be in your bed, too."

"He does?" Trying hard to focus and clear sleep-fog from her brain, Paris looked around the room. It was empty except for her and Elly. "Where is he?"

Elly turned. "He's goned," she said, alarm rising in her voice as she scooted off the bed and hurried from the room.

Paris threw back the covers, grabbed for her robe and rushed after the little girl. She shoved her arms into the sleeves and fumbled for the belt as she shuffled into the hallway. Elly was already in her own room, frantically searching the playpen for her little brother when Paris joined her.

"He's not here," Elly wailed. "Somebody's got him."

"No, no, we'll find him," Paris assured her, sweeping Elly into her arms. The little girl immediately curled her arms around Paris's neck in a stranglehold. A soft cry behind them told her where the little boy was. Paris turned and hurried back to the hallway, where she found Simon sleepily fumbling at the knob of Mac's bedroom door. He couldn't quite reach it, and his groggy efforts were heartrending to see.

Paris rushed to him. "It's okay, Simon. Come with me," she whispered, staggering slightly as Elly's weight around her neck pitched her forward. She stumbled against the door just as it was swept open by Mac. Paris barreled into him.

"Oomph," he grunted, taking the impact of her head against his chest muscles.

Paris bounced back, her ears ringing. Were his pectoral muscles made of iron, she wondered, as she struggled to keep her grip on Elly. Mac's arm shot out automatically to hold the two females upright. His free hand slapped the hall light on and they all squinted in its brightness.

"Oomph," Simon repeated softly, wrapping himself around Mac's legs, then said "oomph" again as if the sound of it pleased him and his fright was forgotten. Calm now, he looked up to see what everyone else was going to do.

"What's going on?" Mac asked, his voice low and knotted with sleep.

"The children woke, and…" Paris began, pushing away from the disturbing strength of his arms and clutching Elly to her like a shield. She wished she had a free hand to smooth her tumbled hair and make sure her knee-length robe covered her decently, then wondered why she cared. No one else did.

"We wanna sleep with you," Elly said, bringing Paris back to the reason for these midnight wanderings. "Me and Simon."

Paris blinked at her. "I thought you wanted to sleep with me."

"Yeah." Elly's tangled curls bounced as she nodded vigorously. "We do. Don't we, Simon? Elly and Simon want to sleep with you."

"Seep," Simon confirmed, and popped his thumb into his mouth.

"You can't have it both ways, Elly. You can either sleep with your Uncle Mac, or with Paris," she pointed out, automatically picking up on Elly's habit of speaking of herself in the third person.

"Unka Mac and Pris," Elly said, nodding as if the adults had finally understood and it was all settled. She lifted herself in Paris's arms and tried to peer past the shoulders that were blocking the doorway. "Let's go."

The four of them in the same bed? Paris's eyes widened then shot from the bed to its owner, who was treating them to his familiar scowl. He didn't seem to like the idea any better than she did. Bolstered, she said, "No, Elly, we can't do that—"

"Why not?" Mac interrupted.

Alarmed, Paris met his gaze. "Why, we just can't, that's all. It would...it would set a bad precedent," she finished lamely.

"It would mean we'd all get some sleep," he responded.

Paris swept a stunned look over his face and across his chest. *Oh yeah?* She barely kept herself from voicing her skepticism aloud. "No, it would be best if I took the children into my bed, and we slept there."

Simon grunted to be picked up. Mac glanced down, looking momentarily baffled, then realized what the boy wanted and bent to lift him into his arms. Simon didn't curl trustingly against Mac the way Elly was doing with Paris, but he did reach out and begin twining his fingers through Mac's chest hairs, plucking at them happily.

"Ouch," Mac said, starting to pull the baby's hand away. Realizing that hurt worse because of Simon's grip, he winced and gingerly peeled the little fingers off instead. He looked from one child to the other. "How about it, kids, do you want to sleep with Paris?"

"No," Elly said firmly. "Pris *and* Mac *and* Elly *and* Simon."

Mac yawned. "Makes sense to me. Come on. There's room for all of us."

He stepped into the room and Paris could see his bed. His room was the only one she hadn't entered that day and she didn't look at it now. Her gaze sought out the bed and stuck there.

Indeed, there was room enough for all of them. It was king-sized with fluffy pillows and a puffy burgundy-colored comforter that had been thrown back in his haste to scramble from bed and see who was at his door.

Room or not, she still didn't want to do this. "I really don't think this is a good idea."

"I've been up almost every night. This is my opportunity to sleep and I'm going to take it. The kids wouldn't sleep with me in here, so I slept on the floor in their room. My back aches from it and I'm by dam…darned going to sleep all night in my own bed if there's any way at all that I can do that. Now drop your objections, don't fear for your chastity, Paris, and get into bed."

Paris opened her mouth to object, but she caught sight of Elly's worried face. The little girl looked as if she thought this was going to escalate into a real argument. Guiltily, Paris realized she was only making this harder. Finally, she answered meekly, "All right. I'll just go turn off the light in my room." She deposited Elly in the middle of the bed, where Mac had also placed Simon, then went back to her room to switch off the light and make sure that her robe was belted snugly and tucked up around her chin as high as possible.

What on earth was she thinking? She couldn't sleep in the same bed with a man she'd only met that day! It was crazy. Unimaginable. Wrong.

She hadn't slept with any man since Keith's death, or any man other than Keith, for that matter. Her hands flew up to her hot cheeks. She didn't want to be that close to Mac, to be that vulnerable. These thoughts ran through her head, convincing her she should reverse her decision and try once again to talk Mac out of this, but when she heard Elly's distressed whimper calling her name, she knew she had to do it.

Wondering how this whole situation had managed to go sideways on her, she went back down the hall to his room, reluctance dragging at her feet. When she reached it, she saw that both children were snuggled in the center of the bed and Elly was looking expectantly at her.

"Come on, Pris. Get in."

Mac stood beside the bed, his arms folded across his chest and his dark gaze on her. If she'd thought him capable of smiling, she would have been suspicious of the twitch of his lips. His dark eyes traveled from her disheveled hair to her knees, which developed some kind of nervous tic that insisted they knock together beneath the hem of her robe. Mentally, Paris forced a little starch into them.

"Yeah," he said at last. "Get in and let's all settle down."

Paris didn't answer, but lifted her chin and gave him a direct look which managed to note and be thankful for the fact that he wore a pair of sweatpants. She intended to keep her robe on. Let him think what he would.

With a nod, she swept the covers back and lay down, though she couldn't relax. He gave her stiff-as-a-board posture a sardonic look as he turned off the bedside lamp. The bed dipped and resettled, then all was quiet.

Paris felt some of the stiffness going out of her spine as Elly scooted in close. She put her arm around the little girl, then reached over to give Simon a reassuring pat. Instead of soft baby skin or a diapered bottom, she encountered the hair-dusted back of Mac's hand which he'd placed over the baby.

Her fingers sprang away and she heard him sigh in annoyance. "Relax, Paris. You're safe here."

Oddly enough, she believed him.

CHAPTER THREE

MAC stood in the master bathroom doorway, rubbing his damp hair with a towel, and marveling at the three people occupying his bed. It had never seemed small before last night, though truthfully, he'd never shared it with anyone before. It had been the one thing he'd bought new when all his other furniture had disappeared along with his ex-fiancée.

The bed seemed crowded now with Paris teetering on one edge, as far from his side as possible and the two babies snuggled up against her, her arm around them in comfort, her bright hair spread over the pillow and hiding her face. Only her chin peeked out as if to lead her through sleep the way it forged her way through life. He had known her less than twenty-four hours, but he'd quickly discovered that he didn't much like being on the receiving end when that chin thrust forward.

What snagged his attention again and again, though, was her hair. He couldn't keep his eyes off it, spilling its red-gold curls against the white pillow slip as if someone had trapped sunshine there.

Mac gave a violent start. *Trapped sunshine?* When had *he* started becoming poetic? Annoyed with himself, Mac shut the bathroom door and finished getting ready for work. The lovely Mrs. Barbour's hair was the last thing he needed to be thinking about right now. He wasn't going to be thinking about her in any way other than as the children's nanny. He was grateful that she'd been willing to accommodate them, and him, last night

by settling in together. She could have fought him on it
even harder than she had, but she'd eventually given in.

He doubted that his solution was the conventional way
the problem of restless and distraught children was usually handled. However, he didn't know much about being a daddy and, in spite of her years of baby-sitting,
she didn't know much about being a nanny. Whatever
method they used to get the children to sleep through
the night seemed okay with him. At least he'd slept
seven hours, more than he'd managed since Elly and
Simon had come to him.

Mac tucked in his shirt, threaded his worn leather belt
through the loops on his jeans, then sat on the side of
the wide Jacuzzi tub and began lacing up his heavy work
boots.

He wondered if the kids had ever climbed into bed
with anyone before. He couldn't imagine Sheila allowing her children to get into bed with her. She wasn't the
most approachable of mothers. In fact, a better word
would be uninterested. It bothered him to think about
the children returning to her. No doubt, she would be no
more interested in them in the future than she had been
in the past. They couldn't stay with him, though. He'd
be even worse for them than Sheila. As careless as she
was, she was still their mother.

Mac pulled his mind from that unproductive thought.
There was no point in taking mental slaps at Sheila. She
was what they'd all made her, him most of all because
he'd wanted to protect their parents from knowledge of
her fecklessness. It worried him deeply, though, because
now there were two children to think of. It had been
different when Sheila had been alone in her flighty be-
havior, but now she was dragging Elly and Simon along
with her. Once she came back and got them, he wouldn't

see them again, probably for months, or until the next time she needed him to care for them. Maybe that wouldn't happen, though. Maybe his little sister would settle down, take the trust fund his parents had set up for her and finish college, make a career for herself and a life for her children.

"Yeah, and maybe pigs will fly," he thought cynically as he left the bathroom and approached the bed. He tried to keep his eyes strictly on the task of scooping up his change and keys from the nightstand and tucking his wallet into his pocket, but his attention strayed to the woman in his bed. He wondered if she'd ever had children. He doubted it because it hadn't been on her resume, and she'd said most of her experience had been in baby-sitting, not raising her own kids.

His lips twitched at the memory of that resume. Damned if he knew why he'd hired her given her minimal experience, but she'd fallen in love with the children right away, her concern for them seeming to spring to life full-blown, unlike his sister who'd had years to nurture her mothering instincts but they were still dead on the vine. He had a good gut instinct and after they'd made it through their original awkwardness yesterday, he'd realized he could trust Paris with the kids.

He left the room, closing the door quietly behind him so that if Simon woke and started wandering, he wouldn't be able to get out without waking Paris, as well. Mac was surprised that he even knew to do that. Before their arrival, he'd never given much thought to the kinds of things a dad needed to do to ensure the safety of his children. Not that he was truly a dad, he corrected himself, or ever would be. Once the kids were gone he'd go back to his solitary lifestyle. He'd learned the hard way that it was best for him and everyone else if he did.

Besides, things were simpler that way. Mac grabbed a jacket and headed out to his truck, locking the house as he went, and ignoring the voice that told him he should be substituting the word *lonelier* for *simpler* in his mind.

Paris woke with a start when a small hand landed on her cheek. Her eyes flew open. Then she relaxed when she realized it was only Simon who had managed to scoot up to the top of the bed and now lay with his head near hers and his arms spread wide. At least he didn't pinch noses like his sister.

Over the months since she'd left Hadley, Paris had developed the habit of keeping her eyes closed for the first few minutes of wakefulness until she remembered exactly where she was.

She didn't need to do that this morning because of the children in the bed beside her and because of the scent that drifted on the air. Mac's aftershave lotion. She'd never smelled it before, but it couldn't be anything else; somehow dark and woodsy overlaid with the tangy scent of the ocean. It was the essence of him.

He must have showered, shaved, and gone to work. It gave her a shiver of unease to realize she had been sleeping as he had moved around the bedroom, gathering his things, perhaps watching her and the children as they slept. At the same time, she felt a sense of unaccustomed serenity at the thought that he had been watching over them, even though he had made it clear that he viewed his role as strictly that of breadwinner and had no intention of being directly involved with the children.

He'd been willing to let the children sleep with him,

she reminded herself, but a cynical little voice also recalled that it was so he could get some sleep himself.

Knowing she probably wasn't going to figure Mac out too quickly, Paris slipped from under Simon's tiny hand and left the room. With any luck, she would have time to shower and dress in the other bathroom down the hall before they woke wanting breakfast.

Ten minutes later she discovered that luck wasn't on her side when the bathroom door banged open. With a startled squeak, she swiped shampoo from her eyes and peeked out from behind the shower curtain to see Elly standing there, holding Simon by the hand.

"Pris?" Elly asked in a fearful tone. "You in there?"

"Yes," Paris answered, pulling the shower curtain around her. "If you two will wait in the hall, I'll be out in a few minutes."

Elly shook her head. "We wait here." She sat down in the middle of the bathroom rug and tugged her little brother down with her. Simon, with his ever-present book under his arm, sat where she indicated, and popped his thumb into his mouth, content to wait.

Flabbergasted, Paris stared at them. They seemed quite determined to stay. Naked and dripping as she was, she had no way to dislodge them. She'd heard it said that mothers of small children forfeited all privacy. No one had ever mentioned that was true of nannies, as well. Resigning herself to her fate, she pulled the curtain shut and quickly finished, rapidly learning that she didn't need all the time she usually took in the shower.

Once she was ready, she began dressing the children and realized that a four-year-old girl has more established fashion opinions than one might have expected. Her clothes had to match and her shoes had to be tied in precise double knots so they wouldn't slip off. Then

Elly had to supervise while Paris dressed Simon, who couldn't have cared less how he looked as long as his precious book was firmly in his grasp.

By the time they were finished, Paris felt as though she needed to stop for a deep breath. She didn't have time to put on makeup or blow-dry her hair as she usually did in an effort to tame the natural curl. Instead, she decided it would have to go wild and she shepherded her little charges to the kitchen where she fixed their breakfast. Glancing around, she saw no evidence that Mac had eaten before he'd left and was saddened by it. No matter what he said, Paris felt that she wasn't earning her salary if he wasn't being provided for, too. However, she wasn't going to talk to him about it again. Instead, she would bake some kind of breakfast rolls and leave them where he could find them. Not that he would probably thank her for the effort, she thought grimly as she sat down at the table and began eating her own breakfast. He certainly seemed determined to accept nothing from her.

"Where's Unka Mac?" Elly asked abruptly, looking up from a piece of pancake she'd been trying to spear with her fork.

"He's gone to work," Paris answered absently.

"Like a daddy?"

Focusing on the little girl's interested face, Paris nodded. "That's right."

"That's what daddies do," Elly said with the air of an expert. "They go to work and the mom and the kids stay home."

Paris grinned. "Have you been watching television shows from the fifties?"

"Huh?"

"Where did you hear this about daddies going to work and everyone else staying home?"

"From Sarah. She's seven. She was my friend at my other house where I lived with my mommy. My mommy went to see elephants and when she gets back she's going to take me and Simon to see them."

Paris's heart sank at the assurance in the little girl's voice, but she could think of no words to answer her. She didn't have to because Elly went on, "Sarah said that daddies go to work. That's what Unka Mac does, but he's not really a daddy."

"Well, no, he's not," Paris admitted, wondering where this was leading.

"He could learn to be a daddy." Elly bumped her feet against the chrome legs of the chair as she considered that. She nodded as if satisfied with her conclusion. "Because he knows how to read."

Paris tried but failed to follow the little girl's reasoning. "What do you mean, Elly?"

"Sarah said her teacher said if you know how to read, you can learn anything." Elly leaned close and spoke in a conspiratorial whisper. "And Unka Mac knows how to read."

Paris bit her lip to keep from laughing at the little girl's serious expression. "Yes," she answered in a choked voice. "He does."

Satisfied, Elly sat back and finished her breakfast while Paris pondered that remarkable conclusion. Remembering her troubling talk with him the night before, she knew it was going to take more than reading ability to make him into a daddy, even a temporary one.

Still, it was worth thinking about. She had been raised to believe it was wrong to try and change another person, that it was unproductive and meddlesome. She hadn't tried to change Keith and she probably should have. His weaknesses had ruined him.

If she hadn't even attempted to change an accommodating man like Keith, she mocked herself, how could she hope to change one like Mac? She thought about the direct way he had of looking at her, of assessing her, of putting up a barrier of stubbornness when she suggested he would want to spend quality time with his niece and nephew. Still, looking at Elly's solemn eyes and Simon's sweet smile, she wished he would try to be closer to them. If what he'd said about their mother was true, and Paris had no reason to doubt it was, then he was the only stable influence they had. They needed him in their lives, just as he needed them.

That day as she moved about his house, she found herself studying the structure as if it held a clue to the man himself. She hardly knew him, but somehow it was hard to equate the stark, colorless interior with him. In spite of his standoffish and solitary attitude, this cold place didn't seem to fit him. She didn't know how she knew that, but she felt as if the place was waiting for warmth and color to invade it. Even if his house begged for warmth, Mac Weston didn't.

As if to put the lie to her thoughts of his solitariness, he surprised her by calling that day. When she answered the ringing phone and heard his voice, she felt her heart stutter and bounce into her throat. Attributing that over-reaction to anxiety about her job, she ignored it.

"How is it going?" he asked and then paused and cleared his throat as if he felt awkward about calling.

Paris gripped the phone, momentarily stumped. What was she supposed to say? *"We're rattling around in this big empty house like three peas in a pod"?* Or maybe, *"We've been holding hands and tiptoeing through rooms to keep down the echoes"?* No. Neither of those replies would further the image of competency she was trying to project.

"Mrs. Barbour?" Mac said sharply. "Paris?"

"Fine," she finally blurted. "Everything here is just fine. The children are fine and I'm..."

"Let me guess," he interrupted dryly. "You're fine, too."

"Yes," she answered, feeling foolish. "I am."

"That's good," he said, sounding not at all reassured. "Any problems?"

She still didn't know exactly what to say so she launched into a description of their morning; bath, dressing, breakfast, and went into such detail that after a few moments, she realized she must sound like an obsessive nut.

"And now, they're watching an educational children's program on television," she finally finished up. "But only for an hour as I don't think too much television is good for children." She then lapsed into silence, half surprised that she didn't hear the sound of his snoring coming over the phone line.

"Um, ah, sounds as though you have everything under control," he said hastily as if he needed to inject words quickly before she launched into a step-by-step description of lunch preparations.

"Yes, I do," she responded with more confidence than she felt. "Do you have any special instructions for me?"

"No, no, do whatever you think is best."

"Yes, I'll do that," she answered, trying to sound as brisk and efficient as any nanny school graduate.

"Yes, well, I'll get back to work now. Goodbye." The phone clicked in her ear and Paris hung up with the feeling that they'd had a conversation that started nowhere, ended nowhere, but somehow left her with the feeling that a tentative foundation had been laid for a bond between him and the children.

Paris couldn't recall ever being the object of such curiosity, she thought as she stared uneasily around the gathering of people in the small market.

Hostility maybe, but not curiosity.

When she had walked in with the children, a few shoppers had glanced her way and fallen silent. Then by some invisible communication, everyone in the place had done the same thing and turned to stare at them.

Nervously, she gripped the children's hands and gave a small smile along with a dip of her head. "Good morning," she said, but her greeting was met with silence. Finally, one woman, a middle-aged lady with tightly curled hair and a pink polyester pantsuit nodded back. "Good morning," she said, giving Paris a careful scrutiny. "I'm Marva Dexter, and you are...?"

Paris blinked at the woman, thinking she was either exceptionally friendly or incredibly nosy. "How do you do?" she stammered in surprise, ignoring the woman's pointed hint for Paris's name.

Paris had grown up in a small town. She knew people there were inquisitive and friendly, but there was something definitely odd about the atmosphere in this store.

Leaving the woman gaping at her and hoping to escape the curious crowd before the children became uncomfortable, Paris quickly grabbed a shopping cart, put Simon into the seat, and Elly into the basket, and began searching for the disposable diapers she'd forgotten to buy the day before in Alban.

In spite of what Mac had said, this place would surely

have diapers in its stock even if it did have customers who'd never seen a stranger before. Not to mention a couple of men in the parking lot who could double as hood ornaments. When she had pulled up, they'd been draped over the fronts of their cars, chatting in a way that told her that was pretty much how they spent their day. Turning to stare at her had probably been the highlight of it, so far.

Paris quickly forgot about those men and the other shoppers as she paused and glanced around with interest. She felt as if she had stepped fifty years back in time. The floor beneath her feet was wooden, worn by many years of feet passing over it. The counters were topped by slate and banded by chrome which shone as if it had been freshly polished. An old-fashioned candy counter displayed the kinds of hard candies and licorice whips her father had once told her about. The store spoke of pride of ownership and Paris felt immediately comfortable. Amused, she wondered if the owner wore a butcher's apron and a paper hat.

She pushed her cart down one aisle and up the next, pointing out interesting items to the children. When she made the next turn, she was surprised to discover the group of customers were still rooted in place, watching with breathless interest as she came around the corner.

This was weird. Paris decided she'd buy her diapers and get out of there.

She must have signaled her intentions because one of the men from the parking lot met her at the other end of the aisle and stood blocking it. The rest of the group gathered behind him to watch her. "You his new woman?"

"Excuse me?" she asked, blinking.

"The king of the hill up there," he said, nodding in

the general direction of Mac's house. "You his new woman? These his kids?"

King of the hill? Seeing the disapproval in his gaze, she drew the cart behind her in order to shield Elly and Simon.

She had no idea what this man was talking about and she didn't want to know. She kept her body between him and the children. Her eyes wide with apprehension, Elly was watching the man's heavy red face. "Excuse me," Paris said in a cold tone as she pushed past him.

The man put his hand out. "Not so fast..."

"Floyd, you wouldn't know fast if it bit you on the butt," a furious voice rapped out.

The man jerked and looked around as the crowd parted and a woman came through.

Paris's mouth dropped open. This was woman with a capital *W*. Tall and statuesque, she had curly black hair that exploded from her head in inky waves and a gorgeous, strong-featured face. She wore practical jeans and a long-sleeved shirt in a warm, inviting shade of tomato red. She swung to a stop in front of the man she'd addressed as Floyd and propped her hands onto her hips in a challenging pose.

Floyd had obviously forgotten whatever he'd been going to say to Paris next because he gulped instead and spoke to the newcomer. "Hello, Becky."

She gave him a dismissive look as she tossed her hair back. "Are you here to shop?" With a wave of her hand, she spoke loudly to the crowd. "I'm happy to have you shop in my store if that's what you're here for, but let's not block the aisle." The crowd drifted away beneath the force of her gaze, but the two men from the parking lot still stood, gaping at Becky as if they were enthralled by her.

Annoyed, she said, "Floyd, don't you and Benny have a car hood somewhere that you need to go dust with your beer bellies?"

Floyd's face reddened. "We were just..."

"On your way out the door."

The one named Benny finally caught on that she didn't want them there. He grabbed Floyd's sleeve and pulled him toward the exit, muttering under his breath.

When the door closed behind them, Becky looked at Paris and smiled. "You'll have to forgive Floyd and Benny. They're mutants who slipped into the Lyte family gene pool while the lifeguard wasn't looking."

Paris laughed, delighted with her and with the way she'd dispatched the two men. She stuck out her hand. "I'm Paris Barbour."

"And I'm Becky Ronson," the other woman answered, giving her hand a shake. "I know about you because Mac called me last night to say he'd found a nanny." Her eyes narrowed and she gave Paris a thorough assessment that made her feel as if she'd been examined from the inside out. Fortunately, she seemed to have passed muster because Becky smiled again.

"You know Mac, then?" Paris asked.

"Sure, my whole life. His sister Sheila and I were best friends until she decided to move to San Francisco and make her mark there. I made mine here."

No kidding, Paris thought, considering the way she had routed those two rude men. This no-nonsense woman wasn't the apron-clad storekeeper she had envisioned.

Becky looked at the children and her face softened. "These are hers. Elly looks exactly like Sheila."

"Peoples tells me that all the time," Elly piped up, making both women laugh. "Pris and Unka Mac are taking care of us 'til she comes back from seeing the elephants.''

Becky cast a swift look at Paris who lifted an eyebrow in a silent shrug.

"Well, that's wonderful," Becky said, recovering quickly. "I bet you'll have lots of fun at Uncle Mac's house."

"Maybe," Elly answered, her little face growing serious. "I don't know yet." As if to end the conversation, she looked away from the two women, placed one arm around her little brother, and hugged her stuffed rabbit with the other.

"It's probably wise to reserve judgment," Becky agreed, then smiled at Paris who smiled back, then grew serious.

"What did that…Floyd person mean? Why would he think I was Mac's 'new woman' and that these are Mac's kids?"

"Because Floyd's an idiot and he doesn't know how to mind his own business. All those other people—well, they're curious because we don't see much of Mac anymore." Becky gave Paris a reassuring smile. "My store is what you might call an unofficial community center. It seems like everyone stops in here at least once a day, but we haven't seen Mac in a while." She clasped her hands together at her waist. "So, what did you come in for today? Maybe I can help you find it."

Surprised by the evasion from this warm and friendly woman, Paris took a moment before she responded that she was looking for diapers for Simon. Becky helped her find them and after she paid, she and the children were soon on their way out the door. Curious stares followed them as they left and Paris couldn't help thinking that there was more going on here than simple curiosity about a reclusive neighbor, but as with Mac and his big, empty house, knew her questions wouldn't be answered soon.

By early evening, the children were drooping and though they tried to stay awake to see Mac, Paris read them their favorite books and put them to bed. As she had promised herself, she baked breakfast rolls and then settled in the big recliner in the family room where she took out her journal and jotted down her thoughts about her first day as a full-time nanny. A lifelong journal-keeper, she was anxious to record her impressions of the day, and especially of the strange reception she'd received in Cliffside.

As she did so, she listened for the sound of Mac's truck, but drifted off to sleep before she heard it.

There were lights on in his house, Mac noticed as he drove along the graveled drive that snaked its way down from the main highway. He couldn't remember the last time he'd come home at night to find lights on. Reminding himself not to get used to it because it was only temporary, Mac stopped the truck in front of the garage and got out, stretching his tired muscles as he did so. He massaged his upper arms, sore from lifting plywood all day and nailing it into place.

A few more months of long days like this and he would be almost out of debt. He could start up his business once again, recoup his losses, rebuild and reclaim his reputation. His life. He gave himself a silent assessment to see if the hard knot of determination that drove him was still riding in his stomach. It was and he was grateful to it because it reminded him that he had only himself to depend on.

He crossed the driveway and opened the back door to

be immediately assaulted by something he'd never smelled there before—baking. The scent of cinnamon swirled on every side of him, setting his mouth to watering. He glanced around quickly and saw the pan of cinnamon rolls cooling on the stove top, waiting to be frosted. He'd never smelled anything so luscious in his life. Unable to resist, he grabbed a knife from a drawer and scooped one out of the pan.

Hot cinnamon and sugar filling oozed out as he bit into it, scorching his tongue. Striding across the kitchen, he grabbed a glass which he filled with milk from the freshly stocked refrigerator, then gulped everything down in a flash. Nothing had ever tasted so wonderful. The tastebuds that had been dulled by the cardboard hamburger he'd bought himself for dinner shot to wakefulness, craving more. That was a command he was happy to obey. He had another roll, and a glass of milk.

With a sigh of satisfaction, he leaned against the counter and thought ruefully that he'd probably consumed his niece and nephew's breakfast, but there seemed to be plenty, and he was too satisfied to feel guilty.

He washed his hands, swiped the coating of sugar and cinnamon from his lips, and thought about the woman who had made the rolls.

In truth, she hadn't been out of his thoughts all day. She'd distracted him while he'd been hammering or sawing, or trying to get the plumb bubble to settle exactly in the center of his level, and he hadn't liked it. He didn't need distractions like the new nanny.

He stepped into the dining room and listened for sounds, then wondered why he felt so disappointed when he heard silence. He only intended to provide material comforts for the children. He didn't mean to get involved with them. If he remained distant, it would be easier when Sheila took them away again.

With that thought ringing in his mind, he stepped into the living room where he saw Paris curled up, asleep in his chair. A book teetered on her knee, ready to drop to the floor. Mac reached for it as it began to slide. Paris must have felt it, too, because she roused and her hand fumbled for the book at the moment his closed around it.

"Oh!" Her eyes shot open and she stared up at him in alarm and her fingers flew up and away from his to hover uncertainly near her face. "Mac." Relief flooded her eyes and then her voice. "I didn't hear you come in. What time is it?"

Because he was busy watching the way she came awake in a rush, uncertainty then comfort washing over her face, his answer was slow to form. When he realized how intently he'd been staring at her, he frowned and stepped back.

"Late," he answered, his voice harsher than he'd intended. "You should be in bed."

She lifted both hands to push her hair away from her face as she yawned, then stood and stretched. "You're right. The kids tried to stay awake so they could say good night to you, but they were too tired. They had a busy day."

Mac dragged his gaze away from the slice of flesh that appeared beneath the hem of the waist-length yellow sweater she wore and a pair of softly worn jeans and frowned even more fiercely. "Don't let them wait up for me. I don't know when I'll be home."

He saw a spark of defiance shoot into the eyes that had been sleepy only moments before, but she obviously reconsidered whatever she'd wanted to say and didn't respond at all.

"What did you do today to make them so tired?" he asked.

Paris picked up the book she'd been reading and a pen she'd dropped on the floor as she told him about a day spent exploring the house, playing with their toys, and walking on the long drive that led from the house to the road.

"Then, before lunch we went in to Cliffside to get more diapers. We met some people who seemed very...curious, and, oh!"

Without thinking, Mac's hand shot out to clasp her shoulder. Dread and fear turned cold, then hot in his mouth. His dark eyes flashed. "What did you say?"

"I...I said we went into Cliffside."

His words were as sharp as a scalpel blade. "I thought I told you not to go there."

CHAPTER FOUR

SHE STARED at him as if he'd lost his mind, and truthfully, he probably had. "No, you didn't. Yesterday you told me to shop in Alban, but I certainly never realized that Cliffside was off limits. This morning on the phone you told me to do whatever I thought was best."

"That didn't include going to Cliffside," he said harshly.

"Well, may I ask why?"

"No." Feeling ridiculous, he snatched his hand off her softly rounded shoulder. "It's just better if you don't go there," he said.

"Not even to shop at Becky Ronson's store? Don't you think that seems a bit extreme?"

"No, I don't," he answered in a gritty tone.

"I don't understand why. She seems to be a friend of yours, and..."

"*Becky* would understand."

"I wish I did," Paris muttered, looking at him in frustration.

"You don't have to understand," he said, stubbornness welling up in him. "You just have to do it."

She lifted a hand as if she intended to snap off a salute, then let it drop to her side. Her shoulders slumped, then squared as she looked up at him. "Yes, sir," she said, and turning, stalked from the room with the short, sharp steps of an angry woman.

Oh, great. He started to go after her, knowing he owed her an explanation, but he stopped himself and turned to the window, his face hard. He'd tried explaining to all and sundry when the world blew up in his face two years ago and no one would listen. They'd been his friends, supposedly, people he'd known his whole life, and they'd been unwilling to hear the truth from him. What made him think this newcomer would listen?

He'd done all the explaining he intended to do.

Paris fumed her way down the hall to her room where she did some agitated back-and-forth pacing, then turned around and fumed her way back to the living room. "King of the hill" as Floyd had called him. "Lord of the manor" was more appropriate. He was carrying bossiness too far. Mac stood in that familiar pose of his, hands in his back pockets, brooding eyes staring into the darkness beyond the huge plate glass windows.

"Why won't you explain?" Paris asked.

Mac turned around. "Which one of us is the employee here, anyway?" he asked.

"You've got the wrong idea about what kind of person I am if you think you can say something like that without a challenge from me."

"Isn't that what a housekeeper/nanny is supposed to do?" he asked stubbornly.

Paris threw her hands out, palm-upward. "How would I know? This is my first housekeeping job, remember?"

"And you're doing a bang-up job, too," he shot back. "Taking two small children where I specifically told you not—"

"You didn't give me any specifics," Paris insisted. "You only told me to shop in Alban for the bulk of the groceries I needed to buy. I had no reason to think I shouldn't go into Cliffside to buy a simple box of diapers."

"Buy the diapers, and everything else you need, in Alban," he responded, pronouncing each syllable clearly. "Since you don't know much about this community or your duties here, why don't you just follow orders until you learn?"

Insulted by his tone and by his insistence that she had deliberately gone against his wishes, Paris said, "Orders? I don't recall receiving any orders. I do recall being told to feed the children whenever they're hungry and to watch out for them in general, just like any responsible adult would do if they had any common sense."

"Which you certainly didn't show by taking them into Cliffside today."

A hot denial shot to Paris's lips, but she bit it back, knowing that her irritation with him would make her say something she would regret. Besides, it would be pointless to remind him, yet again, that he'd told her to do what she thought best. No doubt he'd said that in haste because he'd regretted his impulse to call and had wanted to get off the phone.

To calm herself, Paris took a deep breath. She couldn't remember ever being so annoyed over someone's stubbornness. She had rarely argued with Keith, even when he'd been busy wasting their money away. His stubbornness had taken a different route—agreeing with the last person he talked to and wanting to please them. Keith had been difficult, but this man, she seethed, was impossible.

"You're putting your two-week trial period in jeopardy."

"Oh, really?' she asked in a tone spilling over with her annoyance.

"Yes, if you can't follow orders, then you're not the

one for this job." His brows drew together and he frowned even more fiercely. "I shouldn't have hired you since you have no housekeeping experience...."

"If I'm such a lousy housekeeper, then what's this?" Reaching up, she surprised them both by swiping sugar and cinnamon off his chin. Then, appalled at her temerity, she glanced at the sugar crystals glistening on her thumb.

She didn't know quite where she'd found the nerve to do that. She'd never been confrontational before. She realized to her surprise that she possessed a stubborn streak she'd never suspected. It almost matched Mac's and prompted her to meet his gaze and raise her eyebrows in question.

His dark eyes glinted as they went from her face to the sweet mixture on her thumb and back again. Heat stirred in his eyes. Paris was shocked to realize her irritation was changing into an answering warmth of her own. Where was that unwanted and inappropriate response coming from? Panicked, she fought it down and was grateful when his very next words killed it.

"You're a good baker," he said with a grudging tone that made her tighten her lips. With great care, she dusted the grains from her hand even as she listened to him. "But that doesn't mean you're an expert at anything else and you don't need to be dragging two small children into Cliffside where they might be—" He broke off and his jaw seemed to constrict even more.

Fascinated, Paris waited for him to go on. When he didn't continue, she prompted, "Might be what?" she asked, throwing her hands into the air. "Adored because they're beautiful children? Able to find playmates? Interested in their surroundings? What?"

"Frightened," he rapped out, goaded. He stared at her as if he was daring her to dispute him.

Paris opened her mouth, then closed it again as she thought of Floyd. He appeared to be harmless enough, just had a big mouth. And yet, Elly *had* seemed frightened by him. But Mac didn't know that, so he had something else in mind.

"Why would they be frightened?"

"They've had enough changes thrown at them in the past few days, they don't need to be dragged into town where people will stare at them, make them feel uncomfortable."

That thin explanation told her more about him than it did about his true reasons. He was hiding something. She had already suspected it, but now she was sure. She wanted to ask him what was wrong, what it was that made him so cautious, wary and evasive, but his very evasiveness told her he wouldn't give her a straight answer. One of them needed to back down, and it looked like she was the one. After all, he was the boss. Even with her limited work experience, she knew it was a bad idea to argue with the one who signed her paychecks.

"All right," she said, repressing the paradoxical feeling that even though she knew she shouldn't argue with the boss, she was giving in too easily, just as she always had with Keith. It would help if she knew exactly why he thought the children would be made uncomfortable, but truthfully she already knew that it had something to do with him. "But you might want to consider that if they're with you for very long, they're going to need playmates and those can only be found in town. It would be silly to drive them all the way into Alban for that."

Mac stared at her for several seconds as if weighing her words. "If playmates seem to be necessary, I might reconsider. Right now, they've got each other, and more importantly, they've got you. Don't you think your job should include being a playmate for them, or isn't that included in your job description?''

"I don't know because I don't have a job description, remember?'' she responded, recalling too late that she'd intended to be a little more stingy with her snappy comebacks.

"Well, I guess it's a good thing I've spelled matters out for you, isn't it?'' Mac asked. He was standing with his chin thrust forward and his brows drawn together, not at all the stance of a man who was going to offer more concessions.

A woman with any sense would have backed down from that expression. One part of Paris's mind urged her to be that sensible woman while another part goaded her on.

"What about you?'' she asked.

"What about me?''

"Are you willing to come home and be a playmate and companion for the children?''

"Didn't we have this conversation? I've got to work. If I don't work, none of us eat.''

Paris finally swallowed the reply that rose to her lips, knowing she'd been on the verge of saying something that would really annoy him. Time to back down.

"All right,'' she said, barely rescuing her tone from being snappish.

Her hope was that the situation would change and she would be free to take the children to the park or a play group in town. Barring that, maybe he would tell her why he was so adamant about avoiding Cliffside.

She sneaked a peek at his brooding face and gave an inward sigh. Then again, maybe he would never tell her.

Turning away, she started from the room as she murmured good-night.

"Paris," he called after her.

She glanced back. "Yes?"

He lifted a hand as if he was going to make a conciliatory gesture, then dropped it and shrugged. "If you need help with the children in the night, wake me."

"I don't think that will be necessary," she answered in a tone cooler than she'd intended. "They're used to me now and I think if they become frightened, they'll be willing to come into bed with me or let me sleep in their room. We won't need to disturb you."

His eyes sharpened and for a moment, Paris thought she'd hurt him, but then his face went blank and he nodded. "All right, then. Good night."

Paris went away with the unhappy feeling that she and the children probably wouldn't see much of him if he kept up his practice of leaving early and coming home late. She didn't know if she felt more sorry for them or for herself. No reason to feel sorry for him, though. It was his choice, after all.

Paris stuck close to home with the children for a week, and as she had predicted, she rarely saw Mac. Elly asked about him frequently and Paris made excuses, then was furious with herself for doing so. She knew why he was never around, that he had to work long hours, but that didn't mean she had to condone what she saw as his neglect.

When she prepared dinner for herself and the children, she made a plate for him, too, and left it in the refrigerator. The first three days, she found it, untouched, in the morning, but on the fourth night, she woke to the scent of her meatballs and mushroom gravy being heated in the microwave oven and smiled to herself with a hint of smugness. Maybe she wasn't making progress in drawing him closer to Elly and Simon—after all, how could that happen if he was rarely home? However, she'd interested him in her cooking and maybe he'd be willing to forgo his fast-food dinners to come home and share the meal with his niece and nephew.

Paris's own relationship with them grew stronger each day. Elly talked about her mother and Paris hid her own feelings of anger toward the other woman and listened attentively. She was able to pick up on the kinds of things Elly liked to do with her mother, like brush her hair and "fix" it, so one afternoon she let Elly brush her long hair and twist it up unto little knots held in place with Elly's small plastic barrettes.

Paris, who, in spite of her child-care experience, hadn't known about a little girl's love for beauty routines, looked in a hand mirror and watched her hair being tortured up into improbable twists and loops that continually succumbed to gravity and slid down around her ears. Elly's solution was to stick in another hairpin or barrette until Paris began to look as though she was wired for sound. While all this was going on, Simon climbed into her lap with his books and she had to read to him all the ones she'd read a dozen times already. Fighting a yawn, she decided a trip to the public library was in order.

When Elly was finally satisfied with her work, and Paris was exhausted from sitting for an hour on the floor being fussed over, she scooted plump little Simon off her lap, settled both children in front of an appropriate television program, and stumbled stiffly into the kitchen to start dinner. She peeked in on them every few minutes to see if she could sneak past and return her hair to normal, but Elly looked up and grinned with delight each time Paris glanced her way. Knowing she couldn't crush the little girl's feelings by destroying her new hairdo, Paris only smiled back weakly and resolved to leave things as they were until after the children were in bed. After all, who was going to see her except them?

She was dredging chicken pieces in a flour and herb mixture, preparing them for frying when she received an answer to that question. The back door opened and Mac walked in.

Surprised, Paris whirled around and instinctively threw her hands up to cover her hair, only to remember too late that they were covered with the sticky flour mixture. Specks of it dropped into her hair and scraped off on the edges of the pins and barrettes. "Ooooh," she moaned when she realized what she'd done.

"What the…?" Mac asked, rocking to a stop just inside the door. His gaze swept over her hair and her reddening face, and laughter sparked in his eyes. He crossed the room to stand before her while his amused gaze traveled over her. "What are you supposed to represent?"

"Nothing," Paris said, lifting her chin. "Elly wanted to fix my hair, so I let her. She said she used to do it with her mother all the time."

"Then she's indulging in wishful thinking," Mac said, leaning against the counter beside the spot where she had been working. "There's no way Sheila would allow Elly to do that to her."

Paris, feeling crowded by his solid presence, could think of no reply to his statement about his sister, so she turned to the sink to wash her hands, then went into the bathroom by the back door and began trying to pick the specks of flour mixture out of her hair. She was leaning over the sink so she could see better when she heard Mac step into the room behind her.

"Here, let me," he said, placing his hands on her shoulders and turning her around as if she was no bigger than Elly.

For the second time in the space of five minutes, he had surprised her. Considering the tension that had been between them before, she was taken aback. Her astonishment kept her very still while he pulled the specks of flour from her hair.

Standing with her head bent forward so he could see the top of her hair, Paris had a perfect, close-up view of his strong throat and the V-neck of his shirt. The shirt was chambray, a fabric for which she was suddenly developing a new appreciation because of its soft brushed blue color. Its association with manual labor only served to highlight his masculinity. She watched the way it stretched over his sinewy muscles as he lifted his arms. In fact, she could become truly fond of this material.

She knew he'd been working all day. He should have smelled sweaty and offensive instead of earthy, solid and so real she had the crazy notion that she could lean on his strength and never have to be alone again. Her breath jerked in crookedly at the idea.

"Did I pull your hair?" he asked.

"Nuh, uh, no," she mumbled even as her gaze skidded away from his throat and darted around the floor and the room. She didn't know what had possessed her to even have such a thought unless it was his closeness and her own helpless attraction to him.

"There. All done," he said, and she gulped a lungful of air, grateful for the relief of tension.

"Thank, uh, thank you." She stepped backward, then turned and hurried into the kitchen. Maybe the question wasn't what had possessed her, but what had possessed *him?* He certainly hadn't shown a willingness to be this close to her before.

"You're home early," she said, washing her hands once again and returning to her chore of cooking chicken.

"I quit early because I had to go check on something in Cliffside," he said.

Paris glanced over her shoulder. "I thought you didn't go there."

"I don't unless it's unavoidable, and unfortunately, that's what it was today. Business." He crossed to the refrigerator and took out a can of soda, popped the top open and took a long swallow.

Paris was dying to ask him what kind of business would take him to the town he disliked so much, but she knew he'd probably get that thundercloud look on his face and ignore her question. Instead, she contented herself with a sidelong glance that confirmed for her that her cooking was doing him some good. In the past couple of days she had noticed that he always ate the food she left for him and he couldn't resist the hot rolls and breakfast muffins she made, supposedly for the children, but really to tempt him. His face had lost some of its gauntness and his jeans didn't seem to ride so low on his hips. She was quietly satisfied to know she was helping him whether he wanted her help or not.

The sound of small feet thumping on the floor told her that Elly had been alerted by the popping of the soda can lid and wanted to share. The little girl rushed into the kitchen, followed by Simon, caught sight of her uncle, and squealed, "Unka Mac. You're home!" She dashed across the kitchen, fiery hair bouncing, and threw herself at him.

Obviously stunned by her welcome, Mac could do little except make a grab for her as she leapt upward. She scrambled into his arms and threw her own arms around his neck as she gave him a smacking kiss. "We thought we wasn't going to see you."

Perfect, Paris thought, trying to hide a smile. Elly had said exactly what Paris had been thinking, but in a much more winsome manner.

"Me and Simon missed you," Elly continued. She locked her hands behind his neck and leaned back to grin expectantly into his face.

Mac gave his little niece a surprised look, obviously recalling her usual hesitation around him. Paris was pleased that Elly felt secure enough to approach her uncle with enthusiasm, and she hoped he saw it that way, as well.

His eyes met Paris's over the top of Elly's curly head. She saw gratitude flickering there.

"Uh, well, I missed you, too," Mac said, giving her an awkward pat on the back. "What, uh, have you been doing all day?"

She twisted in his arms and threw her hand out dramatically. "I've been fixing Pris's hair. Doesn't she look beautiful?" She beamed at her handiwork and Paris grinned back, giving a curtsy that made Elly chortle.

"Oh, yes," Mac said, humor lighting his eyes and shimmering in his voice. "Beautiful is exactly the word I would have used for that hairdo."

Paris wrinkled her nose at him. A shared moment of humor spun between them before Mac's eyes darkened a bit and he said, "But what else did you do today, Elly?"

"That's all," she said with a careless shrug. "Pris only lets us watch a little bit of TV. She said too much is bad for us like too much chocolate, but she was just being silly because we can't eat the TV.''

"No, no you can't," he answered thoughtfully, then slanted a glance at Paris. "Too much chocolate?"

Paris lifted one shoulder in a shrug. "Well, it's not very nutritious."

Simon toddled to his uncle, lifted his arms and said, "Up," in a matter-of-fact way. Paris pressed her lips together as she attempted to hide another delighted smile. She wondered if Mac realized the children were so welcoming because they felt more secure in the stable environment he was providing for them.

Mac had to sit down in one of the kitchen chairs in order to hold both children on his knees. Even then, he seemed to keep them at something of a distance, not snuggling them in close as Paris would have done. Still, she thought he was making tremendous progress if only by holding them.

As he balanced the children somewhat awkwardly on his knees, Mac looked up and said, "What else do you do with them, Paris?"

She answered as she turned on the burner under the pan to heat the oil for frying the chicken. "We take lots of walks. We read books. I've begun teaching Elly the alphabet and numbers."

"I can count," Elly said and began a rambling count of numbers where she repeated and backtracked many times, but eventually reached ten. She beamed at her uncle, who gave her a somewhat uncertain smile that made Paris want to giggle.

His bemused expression made her think of an illustration in one of Simon's books where a ferocious tiger was held enthralled by the sight of a butterfly that had landed on his paw.

Mac really was at a loss around the children. She found it charming.

"I guess I didn't realize how they would be affected by living out here," he said slowly. "By having no play-mates."

"They're not suffering," Paris said quickly even as she wondered at the cause of his shift in attitude.

"No, but they need friends."

She couldn't disagree with that since she was the one who had brought the suggestion up in the first place.

"I suppose there's some kind of little kid play group in Alban."

"I'm sure there is. Most communities have such things at the local park or community center."

"You could ask Becky about it."

Paris blinked. "Becky?" she asked cautiously.

"She knows a lot of what's going on all along the coast. She's on the Cliffside city council. She'll know."

"The city council?" Paris thought about the town council members in Hadley, a couple of ladies who knit-ted their way through meetings and three local farmers, each with his own agenda. If Cliffside elected Becky to the town council, there might be more to the town than she'd suspected, which made her all the more curious about why Mac disliked the place so much.

"Yeah," Mac said, misunderstanding her silence. "Even a place as small as Cliffside has a town council, though Becky's probably the only one on it who has much sense."

Despite the fact that Paris wanted to hear more, she only nodded and murmured, "I see."

Obviously thinking he'd revealed too much, Mac's face got the shuttered look that seemed to be second nature to him. He eased the children off his lap and stood as he said, "Anyway, call Becky if you think Elly and Simon need contact with other children. Her number's in the book."

The dispassionate tone of his voice made her pause and meet the coolness in his eyes. The tone he used wasn't uncaring. It was almost…resigned, she decided. A flurry of protectiveness swirled through her, but she couldn't have said if it was for the children or him.

"But you'd still prefer that I not take the children into Cliffside?" she asked, unable to resist the urge to probe.

"You're not being held prisoner here, Paris," he responded dryly. She couldn't think of an answer to that because in a way, she and the children were prisoners of circumstances only he seemed to know—and wouldn't explain.

"I don't want them to miss out on what they need," he said as if the words were being dragged from him. Paris waited and when the silence had stretched for long moments, he continued, "Maybe a short trip into Cliffside."

She blinked at this reversal, but before he could change his mind back again, hastily said, "How about a visit to the public library for new books. If I have to read those books of Simon's again, I'll go bonkers."

Her feeble humor didn't bring a smile to Mac's mouth, but his eyes narrowed slightly as he considered. "All right," he responded in that neutral tone. "You can do that." He turned away. "I'm going to take a shower before dinner."

He walked out, leaving a disappointed Elly behind. Paris sympathized with the little girl. She had some dashed hopes of her own. For a moment there, she'd thought she'd seen a softening in him, but then he'd closed off. Paris knew it had something to do with the decision to let her take the children into Cliffside. She was almost sorry now that she'd pursued it.

To deal with her own guilty feelings, she asked Elly to set the table for the four of them, the first meal they'd shared since Paris had been there. She considered that to be progress.

She knew she should be pleased that he'd agreed to let her find playmates for the children, and take them to the library, but seeing his misgivings, she was beginning to wonder if she was doing the right thing, after all.

CHAPTER FIVE

IN SPITE of her lingering feelings that she had somehow manipulated Mac, Paris took the children to the library in Cliffside where Simon's eyes grew wide with excitement at the sight of all those books. After making some phone calls to confirm that Paris actually lived in the area and wasn't some out-of-town interloper attempting to abscond with books from the Cliffside public library, the woman in charge allowed her to check out almost as many as she and the children could carry.

For herself, Paris found some books on child development and child care that the librarian stamped and then handed over with a smirk. Paris knew the woman was dying to ask about the children, but wasn't quite rude enough to do so in front of them.

With the disgruntled thought that people in Cliffside reminded her a great deal of the citizens in her hometown of Hadley, Paris shepherded the children toward the car. She loaded the books into the backseat, except for the one in Simon's hand. As she turned to put the children into their car seats, she heard Elly squeal, "Swings! Come on, Simon. Let's go swing!"

Before Paris could stop her, Elly was running through the flowerbeds and into the small city park beside the library. "Wait, Elly," she called, slamming the car door and hurrying along behind the little girl who was making a beeline for the playground equipment. Paris snatched up Simon as she went.

Simon reached out and yelled, "Whings! Whings!"

and threw his body around in an attempt to get down and run to them. Paris had to juggle to keep from dropping him.

"Look, Pris, you can push us on the swings!" Elly shrilled, clambering onto one. Her small hands gripped the chains on either side and she looked up excitedly. "Let's go, Simon. Let's go."

Her little brother was all for that idea and once again made a lunge for the ground that had Paris staggering under his weight even as she continued to hurry toward Elly. When she reached her, she set Simon on his feet because she was about to drop him. He trudged toward the nearest swing, grabbed the seat, then looked to her for help when he couldn't climb on by himself.

Momentarily helpless, Paris considered what to do.

Mac had specified a "short trip" into town, and only after much discussion and disagreement. He hadn't authorized a side trip to the park. Paris's first instinct was to pull the children away and take them home, but Simon was eager to swing—so much so that he'd dropped his beloved book in the dirt—and Elly was wild with delight and eagerness, her little face beginning to grow anxious that this treat was going to be denied her. Paris knew she couldn't disappoint them. Surely Mac wouldn't object to this.

She picked Simon up and deposited him in a swing with a baby harness where she gave him a gentle push. He responded with one of his deep-throated chortles. Paris forgot about her momentary worries over what Mac would say. She wasn't trying to defy him, and she couldn't imagine that he would begrudge the children this fun.

Satisfied with that logic, Paris concentrated on playing with them. She pushed the swings and caught the children at the bottom of the slide until her arms ached. As she did so, she couldn't help comparing the satisfied tiredness she felt with the unfulfilling aimlessness she'd known in the years of her marriage to Keith.

Maybe if they'd had children, she thought as she placed Elly and Simon on side-by-side rocking horses and took turns giving them each a push, things might have been different. Maybe Keith would have been less open to scams and sad stories if he'd considered that the loss of the money he was squandering was hurting his children.

Maybe not, though. After all, Keith hadn't listened to her admonishments that he was risking their future. The feeling of loss and sadness that had overwhelmed her for so many months didn't seem quite as devastating just now, standing in the morning sunshine, playing with two children.

She had wandered aimlessly for a year, left behind everything she'd known, taken jobs she never would have imagined herself doing in order to recover from the loss of her husband and get over the disillusionment and disappointment she had felt. None of that had done her as much good as the simple pleasure of caring for these toddlers.

After a few minutes on the horses, the children hurried back to their favorites, the swings.

"Higher, Pris," Elly demanded, bouncing on the swing seat and bringing Paris back to the present. "Higher."

Paris told her to hold on tight, then showed her how to stretch her short, chubby legs out and bring them back in to make herself go higher. Elly was delighted with this new skill and practiced it over and over. Simon was content to swing placidly back and forth, watching the world tilt and change. Occasionally he would give one of his deep laughs at nothing in particular.

Paris's heart swelled with love for the two of them and hard on the heels of that came thoughts of their uncle and her usual feelings of uncertainty.

When he had returned to the kitchen after his shower yesterday evening, there'd been no return of the cautious warmth she'd seen earlier—neither toward her nor the children. By the time dinner and nightly baths were over, and the children were tucked into bed, he had disappeared into his room where she could hear him moving about restlessly.

She had stood for a moment outside his door, wondering if there was something she could say or do to calm him. Appalled at herself, she'd finally fled to her own room. She was taking this whole nanny/housekeeper/caregiver thing too far. Calming the boss was not her job!

Still, calm or stormy, she wished he didn't occupy so much of her thoughts.

It was almost noon by the time she could persuade the children it was time to leave the park, and only accomplished it then by telling them she needed to stop at the store. With thoughts of a possible treat in mind, Elly finally scrambled into the car and buckled herself in, then instructed Paris on how Simon needed to be secured in his seat.

When they arrived at Becky's grocery store, Paris was relieved to see that the two men who'd gaped at her and the children before weren't out front. Of course, that didn't mean they weren't inside. Carrying Simon on her hip, and holding Elly by the hand, she stepped cautiously into the store, then breathed a sigh of relief when it appeared that the place was empty except for Becky, who stood behind the counter, filling glass jars with a colorful array of hard candies.

Becky glanced up when they came in and broke into a big smile.

"Hi! Welcome back." She came from behind the counter to chuck Simon under his double chins and give Elly a gentle pat on the back. "How are you doing?"

Elly ducked behind Paris's skirt, but peeked out and smiled shyly at Becky who took two pieces of candy from her stock and offered them to the children, winning them over instantly.

Paris then asked about play groups for Elly and Simon but before Becky could answer, the old-fashioned bell on the door jingled and a woman strolled in. Becky turned and smiled. "Hi, Mom," she called out, then spoke to Paris. "Paris, this is my mom, June. These are Sheila's children and this is Paris Barbour, who's working for Mac."

June, who was an older, more dignified version of Becky, came over to them. Elly, recognizing a grandmother when she saw one, immediately warmed to the lady, who commented, as Becky had, about how much Elly looked like her mother.

"Can I take them upstairs to your place, Becky? I'd like to call Irene Devlin to come over and meet them. If that's okay with you," June asked Paris. "She was best friends with Mac and Sheila's mother and I know she'd like to see them."

Paris hesitated for a moment, but decided to trust her own judgment. Becky seemed to be Mac's friend, so she thought she could probably trust June, as well. She nodded. "Sure, you can take them upstairs."

June smiled her appreciation and then glanced down at Elly. "Good. We can get a soda," she added by way of inducement for Elly, who nodded vigorously. If Elly was going, Simon placidly toddled along, holding onto June's hand.

Becky watched them leave and smiled. "My brother and his family live in San Francisco, so she doesn't get to see as much of them as she'd like and since I have no intention of becoming a mother, she has to take her grandmotherly pleasures where she can."

Paris laughed at the outspoken honesty. "You don't want children?"

Becky returned to her chore of filling candy jars, but she treated Paris to a teasing look. "What? And interrupt my brilliant career in the retail industry?"

Paris laughed again, enjoying Becky's way of poking fun at herself without apologizing for being satisfied with her life as a small-town shopkeeper.

"Maybe I'll find the right man and have kids someday. How about you?" Becky asked. "What brought you to work for Mac, if you don't mind my asking? And even if you do, answer the question anyway."

Paris gave her an abridged version of the last year of her life, concluding that she wanted a quiet place to work and stay for a while. While she was doing this, another lady walked into the store. Becky introduced her as Irene Devlin. She said hello, then hurried upstairs to meet Sheila's children. Paris was warmed by June and Irene's interest in them.

"Another grandmother on the loose," Becky said, with a grin, then returned to their discussion. "You wanted quiet?" she asked. "Can't get much quieter than Mac's place," Becky said. "Unless the house echoes with no furniture. I just wanted to strangle that spoiled brat Judith for taking everything when she walked out on him."

Judith? Fully alert, Paris moved closer. She didn't want to gossip, or listen to gossip. After all, Mac was her employer. But she truly wanted to know what had made him the cautious, wary man he was and it sounded as though this Judith had something to do with it.

Becky saw the questions in Paris's eyes. "I guess you don't know about her. Mac's not one to talk about himself. If I didn't love him like a brother, I would have kicked him for ever getting involved with that silly woman, but things were going terrifically well for him then. She set her cap for him and she got him. She truly was stunning and I think he was simply dazzled. A wealthy computer engineer hired her to do the interior of a house Mac had designed. That's how they met. We'd never had anything like her in town before, he'd been working long, hard hours without much time to meet any women, worrying over Sheila's marriage because it was coming apart at the seams and Sheila seemed bent on doing every foolish thing that came to mind."

Like leaving her children with Mac and taking off for Africa, Paris thought.

"Judith must have seemed like every man's fantasy come true—beautiful, sophisticated. She had a calmness about her that he must have found refreshing. I don't think he realized for a long time that it was plain old coldness." Becky shook her head as she turned and began returning the filled candy jars to the shelves. "I actually gave him credit for enough sense to see through her, but it took the near tragedy of the collapse to get rid of her."

"Near-tragedy?" Paris asked, alarmed. "Collapse? Mac had a collapse?"

Her startled question had Becky rocking back on her

heels and turning around quickly. "You haven't heard? I can't believe no one in this town has filled you in on all the gory details."

"You're the only person I've really talked to here." Paris didn't mention that until yesterday, Mac had all but forbidden her to come into Cliffside. She had the feeling she was about to learn why.

"Well, thank heavens you're hearing this from me. Otherwise, who knows what kinds of lies you'd have been told." Becky came out from behind the counter, took two bottles of apple-flavored soda from a refrigerated case, and showed Paris to a table and chairs that had been set up in a corner of the store. As they sat, she said, "This is the quietest time of the day for me, so we'll have a few minutes to talk before the lunch crowd arrives." She took a sip from her drink. "No, Mac didn't collapse. The new Cliffside elementary school building did. He was the architect and general contractor on it. The building was about half finished, with the walls up and roof on when it collapsed in the middle of the night."

"What happened?"

"Shoddy work."

"Mac's?" Paris asked the question, but she couldn't believe it.

"No. He'd subcontracted the concrete work out to his best friend, Fred Dexter, who did the worst possible job and pocketed huge profits." Becky shook her head. "I don't know how Fred thought he was going to get away with it, the fool. The only good thing was that it fell down before it was finished and not when it was filled with children."

Paris shuddered at the image Becky's words brought

to mind. "I can't believe Mac knew anything about that."

"Oh, he didn't," Becky said quickly. "Up until then, Fred had always been reliable, produced good work and a good product, but he'd begun gambling, and drinking, and, well…it ruined him."

"And Mac felt responsible?"

"Yes. As general contractor, he felt responsible. He ended up having to pay some of the costs. Sold his business, his vehicles. Everything, really, except his house."

"Wasn't there any insurance?"

"Yes, but by the time the new building was started by a different contractor, costs had risen beyond what the school board had allocated. Mac made up the difference out of his own pocket. He pretty much lost everything; business, reputation, fiancée—not that Judith was any great loss. I'm sure she's moved on to greener pastures by now. Still, he was hurt by the whole thing. The worst part, though, was the way the town's treated him since then."

The bell over the door rang and she glanced up in a distracted way at the incoming customers, then leaned forward to whisper in a bitter voice, "They all seemed to have forgotten he was once the high school football hero, that they couldn't brag enough about him when he was in college making excellent grades every semester, then pulling himself up by his bootstraps after his parents died and he was left with a sister to finish raising and medical bills to pay. He started his own business when he was just twenty-five and provided some much-needed jobs around here."

Becky stood to take care of her customers while Paris sat back and stared, unseeing, at the tabletop. She had no trouble picturing Mac shouldering the responsibility for the ill-fated school building. It sounded as though he'd hardly been at fault, but he probably hadn't seen it that way. He was no stranger to accepting responsibility. After all, he'd been willing to take in his sister's children and provide for them when Sheila got a whim to go on a photographic safari.

Paris felt physically sick as she saw the uncomfortable comparisons between his situation and that of her husband, Keith. For Mac, the town had become his enemy. For Keith, it had robbed him of his wealth and standing in the community—the things he valued most. Although the two men couldn't have been more different, they were alike in the way friends had turned on them.

Engrossed in thought, and wanting to ask Becky more questions, Paris stood and followed her friend through the store. Absently, she rounded the end of an aisle as she said, "But, Becky, Mac couldn't have known what this Fred person was up to, and..."

Her words broke off when she saw that the customers were the Lyte brothers, who turned their heads at the sound of her voice. When they saw who it was, their big bodies lumbered around to face her.

Floyd smirked at her. "Been talking about Mac, huh? And how he tried to kill all the kids in town..."

"Oh, Floyd," Becky broke in furiously, punching his arm as she spoke. "Don't be any more of an idiot than you already are. You know that's not true."

Floyd's moonlike face flushed an ugly shade of purple. "I don't know any such thing."

"You're still mad because he fired your lazy butt before the job even started, and Fred wouldn't hire you, either, so you missed out on honest wages *and* dishonest ones."

"That's not true," he sputtered, his tiny eyes disappearing into slits in his fleshy face. His brother, Benny, chimed in with his own arguments for his brother. While they were quibbling, another customer came in, the older lady Paris had seen in the store before. Marva? Yes, that was her name—Marva Dexter. Oh, Paris thought. Could she be related to Fred?

Marva stopped inside the door and listened to the quarreling for a few minutes before she, too, chimed in, tossing out accusations against Mac that Paris couldn't begin to follow. It was something about Fred being a follower, that Mac had always been the leader in their friendship and that Fred never would have taken such a step if he hadn't been desperate. If Mac had helped him out, Fred wouldn't be in jail, and on and on until Paris's ears were ringing.

Yep, she thought, dazed. Marva was definitely related to Fred, probably his mother.

Becky was too deep in her disagreement with Floyd and Benny to be rational and get the situation under control. Paris could barely understand what they were saying because everyone was talking at once. She held up her hands and shouted. "Wait. Wait a minute here. Listen to yourselves. This can't all be true. There may be a kernel of truth to what you say, but you're contradicting each other and it doesn't make any sense. What did Mac say when you threw these accusations at him?"

"Nothing," Floyd answered in a sulky voice. "He wouldn't say a thing."

"I shouldn't have had to," a deep, intense voice said from behind Paris's shoulder.

With a gasp, Paris whipped around.

Mac, still in his sweat-stained work clothes, stood behind her. His hands were resting at his waist, but she could see the tenseness in his shoulders and the cold light in his eyes, directed straight at her.

"Mac," she said, speaking from a dust-dry throat.

"Mrs. Barbour, where are the children?" he asked in a tone gone dangerously soft.

Paris licked her lips. "They're...they're upstairs with June, uh, Becky's mother."

"I know who June is." His gaze swept the small crowd, which had been frozen in a tableau. Even Becky seemed speechless with surprise. "Why don't you go get them?" he suggested in a way that clearly told her it wasn't a suggestion at all but an order. "It's time to go home."

"All...all right," Paris answered. Blindly, she glanced at Becky. "Thanks for the..." What? she thought wildly. Gossip? Rumors? Chance to get herself fired? "Soda," she finally concluded in a faint voice.

Turning, she hurried toward the back of the store where she found a set of stairs that led up to Becky's apartment. She saw June and Irene emerging with Elly and Simon, both of whom had sticky soda pop stains on their mouths.

Paris mumbled some garbled thanks, scooped up Simon and grabbed Elly's hand. As she turned to leave, she saw Mac waiting at the bottom of the steps. His face was grim and watchful as she descended with the children. Elly started to greet him, but his coldness had her giving him anxious looks and pressing quietly to Paris's side.

"Are you ready?" he asked, still in that deadly tone.

"Uh, yes," Paris said, then cleared her throat. "Yes."

"I guess you got the information you came for?" he asked, his eyes as fathomless as an ocean trench.

No. She'd found out nothing about play groups for

the children, but she nodded, too miserable to try to explain that she'd found information of a completely different sort.

She hustled the children past the people still standing in the store, watching their every move. She kept her chin up and even managed to give Becky a reassuring smile. When she had them safely installed in their car seats, she got behind the wheel and started toward the house on the cliff. The whole time, she was fully aware of Mac, following her silently outside, then sitting with the engine of his truck idling while he waited for her to precede him.

Did he think he had to follow and make sure she didn't make any more stops? Didn't talk to anyone else? Paris gave him a half-annoyed look in her rearview mirror, but her gaze fell away when she saw the set expression on his face. Guilt and feelings of disloyalty pricked at her. She hadn't known exactly why he'd wanted her to avoid the town, but she'd sensed he had a good reason. She hadn't respected that reason because she had been too curious about him and his aversion to Cliffside.

By the time they arrived at the house, Paris was feeling humbled and more than a little apprehensive. She unloaded the children from the car and helped them inside where they, unaware of the tension between the two adults, hurried in to spread out their new library books in the living room and begin looking them over.

Moments later, in the kitchen, Paris turned to face Mac who was quietly seething behind her.

"You couldn't leave it alone, could you?" he asked, his voice low and scathing. "You couldn't just take my word to stay out of Cliffside, could you?"

"I took them to the library as we agreed," Paris said.

"Then Elly saw the swings in the park and wanted to play. Simon wanted to play so badly, and…"

"So you gave in to a baby's *wants?*"

Incensed at his tone, Paris stuck out her chin. "I saw no harm in it."

"Of course you didn't," he said.

"Then, as we had agreed, I stopped to ask Becky about a play group for them."

"You asked a lot more than that, too." He stood towering over her, his dark eyes glaring down at her. "You couldn't wait to go in and find out all you could about me."

"That's not true," Paris shot back, though she knew there was at least a grain of truth in what he said. She might not have brought the subject up, but she hadn't exactly run from the store when Becky had begun telling her about it.

Still, Paris defended herself. "Becky told me what had happened, and I was glad she did because she obviously likes you and is on your side. I would rather have heard it from her than from all those other people."

Mac leaned close and his voice registered a new low of fury. "Since it's really none of your business, Paris, it doesn't much matter who you heard it from."

Hurt and angry, she stepped back. "If it's something that might affect the children in my care, then it's my business. You wouldn't tell me why you had such an aversion to Cliffside, so I had to find out somewhere in case it could harm Elly and Simon."

"Now you know, don't you? It can." Mac looked for a moment as if he wanted to say more, then shook his head and stepped back. Turning, he stalked around the cavernous kitchen before coming back to her. "Did Elly and Simon hear any of what those fool Lyte brothers and Mrs. Dexter had to say?''

''No,'' she answered quickly. ''They were with June the whole time.''

''Well, thank God for that small blessing,'' he muttered.

''Mac,'' Paris said, holding out her hands placatingly. ''This isn't going to affect them.''

''How do you know that? Just how could you possibly know that?'' he asked. ''You don't know what it's like to have things whispered about you.''

Paris stared at him. Oh, yes, she did. The ''friends'' who'd wanted Keith's money hadn't appreciated her attempts to keep him from giving it away. They'd started a devastating whispering campaign about her.

She wasn't going to tell Mac that, though. He wouldn't have cared. After all, she was only an employee. She didn't bother breaking into his monologue.

''I don't mind it for myself, but I don't want it to upset my niece and nephew.''

''They're four years and eighteen months old,'' Paris responded. ''They didn't know what those people were—''

''And that means what?'' he interrupted furiously. ''That they can't understand a vicious tone of voice?''

''Well, I—''

''Haven't they been through enough already by being dumped here by their mother?'' As if he couldn't contain his fury any longer, Mac jerked away, took a few agitated turns around the room, then came back to face her. His hand sliced the air furiously. ''By being left with an uncle they've hardly ever seen, who was stupid enough to hire a nanny who won't follow orders.''

"Now wait a minute," Paris said, as angry now as he was.

"No," he said. "*You* wait a minute. You were wrong and what you did could have hurt them just as much as they've been hurt by being abandoned here by their mother. I'm all they've got left. Don't you see that? They need to know I'll take care of them."

Stricken, Paris gazed at him. She hadn't considered that as carefully as she should have. "Oh," she murmured. "I didn't think—"

"No, you didn't." Mac's big, calloused hand sliced the air once again to cut her off. "And that's why you're fired."

CHAPTER SIX

"FIRED?" Paris stared at him, her green eyes wide, stunned.

"That's right." Mac turned, paced away, then came back. He hadn't been this furious with anyone in years. Even when he'd found out his foolish friend Fred had cheated him and ruined his business, Mac hadn't been this angry. Somehow with Paris, though, he felt what she'd done was worse than Fred's foolishness and dishonesty. It was a betrayal. He wasn't going to think about the reasons behind that feeling, though. He was going to get rid of her. He'd had enough betrayals in his life, and he wasn't going to let this affect Elly and Simon.

"Yes, fired," he rapped out each syllable as if he was spitting bullets. "If you can't do what you're supposed to do, if you can't follow orders, you don't need to be working for me. You're not the right person for the job."

Paris gulped in air. Since she'd never had a job before, he knew she'd never been fired before, but it wasn't hard to see she didn't like it. Too bad. She should have thought of that before she'd exposed his niece and nephew to risk.

"But I had a two-week trial, and…"

"It's canceled," he snapped.

She held up her hand. "Wait a minute, Mac. I made a mistake, sure, but there's no harm done. The children didn't suffer, and if you'll recall, you're the one who told me to ask Becky about a play group for the kids."

"I said for you to *call* her, not drag the children into a hostile situation."

"Hostile?" He saw annoyance spark in her eyes as she put her hands on her hips and stared at him.

"Oh, don't sound so innocent," he scoffed. "You can't tell me that wasn't hostility I walked into in that store."

"You maybe, but not the children. Becky and June couldn't have been nicer to them, and I'm sure the other lady who came to see them, Irene, was kind to them as well or they wouldn't have looked so happy when I went to pick them up."

His hand shot out and he held up three fingers. "Three people. Three people in a town of a thousand are nice to them." Momentarily, his irritation burned away his power of speech and he took another sharp turn around the room.

He had to get his fury under control, he thought, or he was going to lose his temper completely. He took a breath and tried to calm himself by avoiding her eyes and staring around the stark kitchen.

In spite of his anger, he noticed that in the past week the place had undergone a transformation. It no longer had the look of an operating room. His distracted gaze managed to note the wildflowers she and the children had picked and stuck into jars and cans which now dotted the barren surfaces with sparks of warmth. Stalks of Monterey Paintbrush bobbed their red heads in an empty tomato sauce can, echoing the color in the dinette set.

Paris had obviously tried to fix the place up, make it livable, which said she cared about it, about the children. So why had she done this? Why had she ruined everything by dragging up the past he was trying to put behind him?

"Does it occur to you that maybe you're overreacting?" she asked, breaking into his thoughts.

He stopped his pacing and turned around so fast, his feet scraped the floor. "No, it doesn't because I'm not. You did exactly what I asked you not to do, so you're fired."

"Pris is afired?" Elly's voice spoke from the kitchen doorway and Mac spun around to see her standing there, clutching a book. It dropped to the floor as her small hands went lax, her shoulders slumped and her bottom lip began to quiver. Big blue eyes were wide with alarm.

Mac's haze of anger with Paris began to clear as he focused on his niece.

"Elly," he began holding out his hand helplessly, knowing it was an inadequate gesture. Not to mention inept. "Listen to me."

"Mrs. Stone was afired," she said, her gaze going from him to Paris and back. "Her whole apartment was fired."

"Fired?" he asked, trying to twist his thoughts with hers and figure out what she was talking about. Whatever it was, she was terrified of it.

Paris figured it out much more quickly than he did and rushed to the little girl. She did a quick twirl in front of her so Elly could see her from all sides. "No, no, sweetie. I'm not on fire." Paris scooped her into her arms.

"Mrs. Stone's kitty almost got fired. It was in her 'partment. The firemen came and poured on water and then the kitty came out. He ran away and Mrs. Stone never found him." Elly's bottom lip began to tremble. "Simon was real scared. He cried."

Devastated, Mac stared at his niece. Paris held her close, kissed her cheek and wiped away tears with a napkin she plucked from the holder on the table. She murmured gentle words to soothe the little girl while Mac stood by helplessly.

"Who was Mrs. Stone, Elly? A neighbor of yours?" Paris asked, nuzzling Elly's coppery hair with her nose.

"Yeah, her 'partment was by ours. There was smoke and fire and we coughed and coughed. Simon was scared," she said again. "Me, too."

"Oh, I'm so sorry, sweetheart," Paris murmured. "But I'll bet your mommy got you away safely, didn't she?"

Elly nodded and buried her face against Paris's neck.

Watching the gentle tenderness with which Paris treated Elly's fears made something crack inside him. She cared so much about them. He still felt angry with her, but was torn by the compassion she was showing Elly.

Mac knew that in spite of his doubts about her, he couldn't do this. He couldn't see such a little one suffer by taking away the most stable person in her life. He'd said it himself, that she'd been through enough. Unwittingly, he'd added to her terrors. What was more, his tiny niece had been in danger and he hadn't known about it, danger far worse than hearing malicious gossip about her uncle.

When had the fire happened? And why hadn't Sheila mentioned it?

Awkwardly, he approached the woman and child and reached out to pat Elly's back, his big, rough hand almost spanning the width.

Unexpectedly, Elly turned and made a lunge for him, winding her arm around his neck when he bent close. She didn't let go of Paris, though, so the two of them nearly bumped noses as Elly pulled them together with a surprisingly strong grasp.

"I don't want Pris to be fired," Elly said, rubbing her forehead against his.

Mac looked into Paris's eyes only millimeters from his. He'd never noticed before that her eyes were flecked with gold, but he could see it, up close like this. Her lashes framed her eyes in feathery spikes, her brows were delicate curves of golden brown. Her skin was smooth and as fine-grained as the Dutch porcelain his mother had once collected.

He didn't want to see all that, to couple it with the love she had for Elly and Simon and the compassion she showed them. Showed him.

The crack that had formed in his gut over his niece's distress seemed to widen. To his discomfort, he felt warmth spark in him, then a tightness in his chest that threatened to squeeze off his air. He didn't need this and he *really* didn't want this, he thought, panic beating at his throat, but he couldn't seem to jerk away.

Elly's tearful voice spoke in his ear. "So Pris isn't afired, Unka Mac?"

"What?" he asked, turning his head to focus on Elly. She didn't know it, but she had him over a barrel. "No," he finally said. "No, she's not."

"Good," Elly said with a satisfied nod, glad to have gotten what she wanted. She wiggled to be let down and they set her on her feet. "I'll go tell Simon. He was scared, too." Before she left the room, she shook her finger at her uncle, and said, "Unka Mac, you yelled at Pris. You should hug her and say you're sorry." Red hair flying, she whirled around and rushed out to find Simon.

"I'm supposed to hug you and say I'm sorry," Mac said, watching the emotions chase across Paris's face.

Paris licked her bottom lip. "No, that's not necessary...."

"But she wants me to." The idea of getting his arms around her was growing more and more appealing by the moment.

"You're...you're the one who said I shouldn't have given in to Simon's wants, and now you're going to give in to Elly's."

"Maybe I'm only trying to understand how the children coerced you into staying in town, going to Becky's, and all the rest of it, when I'd told you to take them to the library and *call* Becky."

She shook her head, annoyance flaring in her eyes. "That doesn't make sense."

"Let's see," Mac said, deviltry lighting his eyes. He put his arms around Paris's slim waist and drew her close. Her soft body pressed against his side and the warmth that had sparked in him burst into heat.

For a moment, he stopped fighting it as he looked down into her eyes. His gaze traveled down to her lips, which had trembled open. Her breath came in soft, shallow puffs that stirred against his chin.

Paris started to pull away, but Mac drew her closer. The press of her soft breasts against him sent his blood pressure soaring and he couldn't recall what they'd been arguing about before Elly had come in. He couldn't remember why he'd been furious with her. In fact, his mind went blank and he had a hard time remembering anything, even his own name. The only thing he could remember was how she felt in his arms. It had been a long, long time since he'd held a woman like this.

The alarm in her eyes, the softness of her face, had

fierce desire mixed with protectiveness bursting open inside him. If he had any reason left, he'd run screaming
from the room. Some candid part of his consciousness
stood back and calmly informed him that he was losing
his mind. Yeah, he knew that already.

"What's the matter, Pris?" he asked. "Afraid?"

That challenge made her angry and brought her chin
up sharply which was perfect because it set her mouth
at the right angle for what he intended.

Her lips were soft, moist. Exquisite. Her taste was
sweet and warm, moving through him and filling his
head. The rational corner of his brain that told him he
was losing his mind prompted him to pull away, to remember this was inappropriate behaviour, but the needy
hunger he'd denied for so long drowned out that sensible
advice and when her lips trembled beneath his, reason
was defeated by a greedy demand for more.

He wanted to crush her mouth against his, feel and
hear her moans of desire, of fulfillment. He wanted...

"No," Paris said, pulling away.

They surfaced, gasping as their lips parted. They
stared, stunned, into each other's eyes. He saw a flare
of panic in Paris's that matched his own. A hug, Elly
had said, and an apology.

He'd almost turned it into a conflagration. He'd been
seduced by that mouth, that soft tenderness.

He stood, pulling air into his lungs as he tried to get
the world to stop rocking beneath his feet. Paris's arms
fell to her sides as if her hands were too heavy to hold
up. Her face was stricken and he knew he ought to say
something, but his power of speech had dried up and
blown away along with his common sense.

He scraped his tongue across his lips. "Paris, I...

You're, you're not fired." His words faltered and he
tried again. "We can work something out...."

Her head snapped back and her eyes filled with something he couldn't read; fear, outrage. He couldn't tell,
but it told him he'd said the wrong thing.

"I've got to go put the kids down for a nap." Paris
said, then turned and fled through the doorway.

Left alone, Mac stumbled backwards and slumped
against the counter. What had he done? What on earth
had he done? He'd changed everything, ruined everything. Now she wasn't the nanny, the housekeeper, the
hired help anymore. Paris was a woman and he was all
too aware of it.

What had he done? Paris asked herself frantically as she
dashed through the house, taking Elly's hand and snatching up Simon as she went. He wailed in protest at her
unexpected swoop and grabbed for his books as she
hauled him aloft. She comforted him with soft murmurs
even as her mind raced and her feet scurried down the
hall to her bedroom.

Mac had ruined everything, she thought, dismayed. It
had been one thing for her to see him as her employer,
even as a man in need of some kind of inner healing,
but to have kissed him, to have responded the way she
did, that was something else, something bigger and more
overwhelming than she wanted to consider.

She had sensed his need, even seen it in his reluctance
to become too attached to his sister's children, but now
she'd actually felt it, tasted it in the desperate moment
of his kiss.

For all of her high-minded thoughts about getting Mac
to bond with his niece and nephew, she'd never seen
herself as part of it. She wanted him to get closer to Elly

Here's a **HOT** offer for you!

Get set for a sizzling summer read...

with **2 FREE ROMANCE BOOKS** and a **FREE MYSTERY GIFT!**

NO CATCH! NO OBLIGATION TO BUY!

Simply complete and return this card and you'll get **2 FREE BOOKS** and **A FREE GIFT** – yours to keep!

Visit us online at www.eHarlequin.com

- The first shipment is yours to keep, absolutely free!
- Enjoy the convenience of Harlequin Romance® books delivered right to your door, before they're available in stores!
- Take advantage of special low pricing for Reader Service Members only!
- After receiving your free books we hope you'll want to remain a subscriber. But the choice is always yours—to continue or cancel, any time at all! So why not take us up on this fabulous invitation, with no risk of any kind. You'll be glad you did!

316 HDL C26A

116 HDL C25Z
(H-R-OS-06/00)

▼ DETACH HERE AND MAIL CARD TODAY! ▼

Name: _____
(Please Print)
Address: _____ Apt.#: _____

City: _____

State/Prov.: _____ Zip/Postal Code: _____

The Harlequin Reader Service® —Here's how it works:

Accepting your 2 free books and gift places you under no obligation to buy anything. You may keep the books and gift and return the shipping statement marked "cancel." If you do not cancel, about a month later we'll send you 6 additional novels and bill you just $2.90 each in the U.S., or $3.34 each in Canada, plus 25¢ delivery per book and applicable taxes if any.* That's the complete price and — compared to cover prices of $3.50 each in the U.S. and $3.99 each in Canada — it's quite a bargain! You may cancel at any time, but if you choose to continue, every month we'll send you 6 more books, which you may either purchase at the discount price or return to us and cancel your subscription.

*Terms and prices subject to change without notice. Sales tax applicable in N.Y. Canadian residents will be charged applicable provincial taxes and GST.

If offer card is missing write to: Harlequin Reader Service, 3010 Walden Ave., P.O. Box 1867, Buffalo, NY 14240-1867

BUSINESS REPLY MAIL
FIRST-CLASS MAIL   PERMIT NO. 717   BUFFALO, NY

POSTAGE WILL BE PAID BY ADDRESSEE

HARLEQUIN READER SERVICE
3010 WALDEN AVE
PO BOX 1867
BUFFALO NY 14240-9952

NO POSTAGE
NECESSARY
IF MAILED
IN THE
UNITED STATES

and Simon, to be part of their lives and let them be part of his, not to make herself part of his life—certainly not to make herself feel anything for him beyond kindness and compassion. There'd been nothing of kindness and compassion in that kiss, though. There'd been only pure need, even lust.

We can work something out. What had he meant by that? Her ambitious imagination had immediately blossomed with sensual images of the two of them, but he probably hadn't meant that at all. No doubt, she was building things up in her mind unnecessarily.

Distraught, barely able to concentrate, Paris climbed onto her bed and snuggled a child on each side of her as she picked the top book from the stack. After a few deep breaths that had both children looking up at her curiously, she managed to calm down and begin reading about a curious monkey who got himself into unbelievable scrapes. Her mind wasn't on the monkey's antics, though, but on Mac's.

He'd been furious with her, tried to fire her, probably rightly so, but Elly had prevented that. Ruefully, Paris glanced at the curly head that rested against her shoulder. The child didn't have any idea how she had changed things by her insistence on a hug. To make it worse, Mac had turned what should have been a simple apology into a bonfire that had scorched them both—and Paris had willingly leaped into it.

They would have to talk about this, she decided. There would be no repeat of it, and she would tell him that in the firmest possible terms. That decided, her insides still quaking, she finished reading to the children who began to nod off before she finished the last book. When they were napping soundly, she left them secure on her bed with pillows tucked around them and went in search of

Mac, but she found the house was empty. He'd driven off in his truck while she'd been with the children.

That was fine, she decided. She would have the rest of the day to formulate what she intended to say. Deep in thought, she stood for a long time at the back door, gazing up the long drive in the direction he had taken.

She might as well have saved herself the trouble of preparing her little speech, she decided by ten o'clock that night. He hadn't come home to hear her deliver it. She had cooked dinner, fed and bathed the children, played with them, read yet more books, and he still hadn't arrived. She killed some time by preparing a lunch for him, bagging it in a paper sack since he didn't seem to own a lunch box, and even wrote his name on the front so he couldn't miss it. Still, he didn't come home.

Irritated, she went to bed, but couldn't sleep until she heard his truck arrive, then the soft sounds of his movements about the house. She considered getting up and speaking to him right then, but hesitated because without the buffer of the children between them, she didn't know what would happen.

"Yeah, right," she muttered to herself, then flopped over onto her stomach and buried her face in her pillow. Her starved libido might lift its treacherous head again and she'd throw herself at him.

She heard Mac go into his room and she twisted onto her back. She had to face facts, she decided, reaching beneath her head and punching up her pillow. It was up to her to put things back the way they'd been, to establish boundaries for their boss/employee relationship that wouldn't accept or permit any more lapses like today.

He hadn't been wrong in his anger. She should have clarified exactly what a "short" trip into Cliffside would be. She had assumed it was okay because it seemed perfectly normal to her, but his strenuous objections and attempt to fire her had told her Mac had a different view. She needed to consider that carefully from now on.

That was it, she decided, relieved. She simply had to make sure they communicated thoroughly on everything to do with the children. They would have that in common, and nothing else. And most importantly, she would keep her lips to herself.

Paris slept badly and rose early so she could talk to Mac before he left for work, but he beat her to it. His truck was disappearing up the driveway by the time she reached the back door.

"For a big man, he sure can move," she muttered. "Either he's got to be at work early, or he doesn't want to face me." She turned to make coffee. When the phone rang, she gave it a surprised look. She'd seldom heard the phone ring in this house.

She scooped it up and was greeted by a faint crackling. "Hello, this is the Weston household. Paris Barbour speaking."

"Paris who...?" a hesitant voice asked. "Uh, this is Sheila White. Is Mac there?"

Paris straightened. Sheila! "No, I'm afraid he isn't, Mrs. White. He just left for work."

"Oh, I thought I'd be able to catch him before he left." Sheila's voice dropped in disappointment. "Who are you? Are you taking care of Elly and Simon?" Her voice faded away completely on the last word.

"Yes, I'm the housekeeper and nanny," Paris answered, glancing behind her to make sure the children weren't awake. She didn't know quite how to handle this call from their mother, but she didn't want them to over-hear.

"Are...are they okay?" Sheila asked.

Sheila sounded as if that was something she thought she was supposed to ask rather than a true concern. Paris frowned, dismayed by her uncharitable thought.

"Both children are fine, Mrs. White."

"Let me talk to Elly."

Heartsick, Paris thought about the way Elly had cried for her mother. She was just beginning to settle down. Paris heartily wished that Mac was here to tell her what to say, then gave a slight start when she realized she was thinking of him as someone to depend on rather than a puzzle to solve.

"I'm afraid both children are still asleep," she said slowly. "But I assure you they're just fine."

"Oh, I see." She paused for several long seconds. "I needed to talk to Mac about something...."

"Shall I have him call you back?"

"No. We've been in Nairobi, but we're leaving. I'll have to call him back when I can, but it won't be for a few days."

A long, awkward pause followed. Paris wondered why Sheila didn't come home and take care of her children if she was so worried about them, then realized guiltily that she didn't want Sheila to come home quite yet be-cause Paris loved Elly and Simon and wanted to stay with them.

Also, she wanted to stay in Mac's house. With Mac.

Sheila cleared her throat. "Do...do they ask about me?" she wanted to know.

"Yes, they do," Paris admitted honestly. "They miss you very much."

"Oh." A long pause followed. "Have you had much experience in caring for children?"

Paris might have laughed if she hadn't been swept with a wave of compassion. Was she thinking she'd made a mistake in leaving her children? That perhaps they were being cared for by an incompetent caregiver? She should have thought about that a couple of weeks ago, but Paris wasn't cruel enough to say so.

"Don't worry," Paris said, trying to project warmth and understanding across thousands of miles. "I've cared for children before and your brother was very careful to check my background and references." That was true, and Paris saw no reason to mention her child-care experience was somewhat limited and panic the woman. "I'm getting along fine with them and they're thriving." Briefly, she told Sheila what the children had been doing, and that they were settling into Mac's home.

"That, that sounds fine, Ms. Barbour. I'm glad they're well...and happy. And not crying," Sheila said. "I really hated it when they cried."

Annoyance sparked sharpness into Paris's voice. "Children do that, Mrs. White. They outgrow it eventually."

"Yeah, I guess so, but I needed a break from it, you know?"

Paris was angry and at a loss to understand such selfishness.

"No," she answered coolly. "I guess I don't."

Even across thousands of miles, Sheila must have understood what that tone meant. She cleared her throat and continued. "Tell Mac I called and I'll call again soon." She hung up before Paris could respond.

Setting the phone back on its cradle, Paris frowned, wondering what Sheila's thoughts were at this moment.

Was she regretting her trip? Missing her children? Had her flightiness taken her farther afield than she'd planned? Or was she just putting on a front of motherly concern? There hadn't been much concern in her voice.

Feeling depressed and sad for Elly and Simon, she opened the refrigerator to begin breakfast preparations and saw the lunch she'd fixed for Mac still sitting on the shelf.

She stared at it for a few seconds, then closed the refrigerator door angrily. She wanted to think he hadn't seen it. Snatching the door open so quickly the condiment bottles rattled, she looked in again and saw that some of the milk in the gallon jug had been drunk. He'd obviously opened the refrigerator at some point. Did he think eating a lunch she'd fixed might constitute some kind of commitment? A long-term relationship?

She was the housekeeper, for heaven's sake. She was *supposed* to fix his lunch, whether he agreed with that or not. Paris sat down at the kitchen table and propped her chin on her hand.

What was with this family, anyway? Sheila runs off and leaves her children then barely sounds as if she regrets it. Says, in fact, that she needs a break from them and their crying. Did she think that was all there was to her children, crying? Did she think that dealing with it was all there was to motherhood?

Paris was at a loss, especially since Elly and Simon didn't cry very much, anyway.

And then there was Mac. He gave the children all the care they needed, but it had taken him a while to bond with them.

He hires a housekeeper, kisses her breathless, but doesn't want her to do anything for him she was hired to do....

"G'mornin', Pris," a sleepy voice said, breaking into her thoughts.

Paris turned quickly to see Elly pad into the kitchen. She held out her arms and Elly came to her, happy to sit on Paris's lap for a few minutes until she was fully awake. Around a yawn, Elly asked, "What are we gonna do today? Can we go back to the park?"

"Well, probably not to the park, but..." Paris paused as she thought about the left-behind lunch. "How would you like to go see your Uncle Mac at lunchtime? We can have a picnic."

CHAPTER SEVEN

MAC wrapped his legs around the edge of a roof beam and leaned forward to pound nails into the plywood he was installing on the roof. Within a few days, they would be ready to begin shingling, he thought with satisfaction as he scooted back and stood, balancing himself easily. He slipped his hammer into the loop on his tool belt, then turned and walked the beam to the ladder he'd used to climb up. Before he descended, he stopped to admire the ocean view.

This was a perfect spot for a house, one of the few undeveloped sites along the coast. The owner, an actor from Los Angeles, had bought the lots on both sides in order to insure his privacy, and had paid a premium price for them. The house was premium, too, earthquake-proofed and built of the best materials, though Mac wasn't sure he agreed with the design. If he'd been the architect on the job, he would have tried to convince the owner that he would like a deck overlooking the ocean, along with the huge windows that invited the outdoors in. However, Mac had heard, and found it highly ironic that the actor, famous for his daredevil action rôles, was afraid of heights. No doubt he felt safer with a wall of windows between himself and the edge of the cliff.

But he wasn't the architect, he reminded himself, continuing his descent down the ladder. He was only a carpenter on this job, thanks to his old friend Jeff Gallo, the contractor, who had put Mac in charge and was giving him the opportunity to rebuild his reputation. It was a strange twist of fate because, at one time, they'd been equals; architect and contractor working together. They would be again. In the meantime, Mac was grateful for the chance and for Jeff's faith in him. The job was coming together beautifully and the men worked well together, spurred by Mac's leadership and by the bonus the owner had promised if the job was finished on time.

Mac smiled grimly. Money spoke. He knew that better than anybody. This time, though, it was going to work to his benefit.

He flexed his shoulders and enjoyed the pleasant tiredness that the morning's work had brought. He felt sorry for anyone who worked indoors on a day like this. In fact, he also felt sorry for anyone who wasn't their own boss, himself included. That was going to change soon, though, and he would once again be sending business to Jeff rather than being hired by his old friend. He'd be out of debt and able to afford a few creature comforts, like furniture. That would please Paris.

Jolted, he stopped. When had he begun thinking in terms of pleasing Paris? He frowned. Oh yeah, he remembered. He'd begun wanting to please her right after he'd made a jackass of himself. It hadn't been the kiss. That had been an error in judgment. He'd begun acting like a fool when he'd run and ducked and hid away from her. Incredible. He'd never run from a challenge in his life, but this woman, with her sassy mouth and begging-to-be-touched hair was scaring the daylights out of him, sending him scuttling from his own house in an effort to avoid her.

Who'd have thought that Mr. and Mrs. Weston's bright boy would turn out to be a coward?

Disgusted with himself, Mac pushed those thoughts aside and focused on a more immediate problem.

Hunger. He'd have to go into Alban to buy something, and would be half-starved by the time he ate.

"Stubborn," he muttered to himself, as he reached the ground level. "Stupid and stubborn." He should have taken the lunch Paris had packed for him, but he'd picked it up, imagined the care she'd taken in preparing it, the same care she used in everything she did for him and the children, and had felt like a fool for having tried to fire her.

He felt like even more of a fool for having kissed her. Somehow, bringing along the lunch she'd packed for him made it seem like he was taking advantage of her, taking her for granted in a kind of kiss-me-today-pack-my-lunch-tomorrow trade-off.

Which, of course, didn't make a speck of sense. But then, his thinking hadn't been sensible for several days now. With a disgusted noise, Mac took off his heavy tool belt and crossed to the sawhorse topped by boards that the men used for a work table.

Beside him, Grey Taggart laid down his own tool belt and gave a long, low whistle. "Damn, who do you think that is? And what's she doing here? Looking for directions maybe."

Mac looked up expecting to see a bikini-clad beach babe trespassing on her way to the public path down the cliff face to the sand.

Instead, he saw Paris standing beside her car, shielding her eyes from the sun as she gazed up at the house. The wind whipped her red-gold hair around her face causing her to reach up with both hands to anchor it. She wore a pumpkin-colored shirt and one of her long skirts, this one patterned with autumn leaves. The breeze plastered her clothes to the front of her body, giving clear delineation to her breasts and the long, supple form of her legs.

Unbidden, a hot lump rose in Mac's throat, then sank, slowly and inexorably to settle low in his stomach where it mutated into desire. He drew in a breath that sounded like a wheeze.

Grey glanced at him and grinned. "Nice, huh? The view certainly is improving around here."

Mac, his eyes fixed on Paris, was having a hard time forming words, but he managed to say, "Grey," in a warning tone.

"Forget it, buddy. I saw her first," Grey answered blithely. "And, hey, she likes what she's seeing, too. She's waving at me." Quickly, he removed his San Francisco Giants baseball cap, smoothed his hair, and resettled the cap on his head. For good measure, he rolled up the sleeves of his T-shirt so his muscles would show. "Do you think this could be my lucky day?"

"Only if she's blind," Mac growled. "And has lost her mind." He started forward. Grey was right on his heels, but he ignored him. What was Paris doing here? Was something wrong? Where were the kids?

He needn't have bothered asking that question because it was answered as soon as it formed in his mind. She opened the back door and began unstrapping them from their car seats. Elly bounced out and ran toward him as fast as her chubby legs could carry her, arms uplifted, shrieking all the way.

"Mac?" Grey asked, rocking back on his heels and giving his friend a speculative look. "You been up to something we don't know about?"

"Probably," Mac said, then grunted when Elly bounced against his knees. He bent to pick her up. She threw her arms around his neck and squeezed tight.

"We're gonna have a picnic," she squealed in his ear, almost causing instant deafness. "We brought samiches and juice and Pris made bwownies. They smelled soooo yummy." Dramatically, she flopped over in his arms to show how the treats had affected her. She giggled when he groaned at the shift in her weight.

Taken aback, but touched by her enthusiastic greeting, Mac could only grab at her to keep her from falling, then bend down to lift Simon who had toddled forward and held his arms to be picked up. Struggling to lift their weight, he straightened and watched as Paris took a blanket from the car and draped it daintily over her arm, then followed that with a large paper sack. After closing and locking the doors, she slipped her keys into her pocket and turned to walk toward him. She continued to hold her hair back with her free hand as she surveyed the ground to see where she was stepping.

The breeze caught her skirt once again and whipped it high above her knees.

"Give me strength," Grey breathed in a barely audible voice. "I wonder what guy's crazy enough to let her out loose. Look at those legs."

Don't you dare, Mac thought, then was jolted by the possessiveness that swept through him. Instead of following his first instinct which was to set the children on the ground and deck Grey, Mac frowned at Paris.

"Why didn't you wear a coat?" he asked when she got within earshot. A long one that reached the ground and buttoned up all the way to her neck, military-style.

She gave him a stunned look. "A coat? It's seventy-five degrees out here, Mac. Why would I wear a coat?"

He couldn't answer that without sounding like a fool. He clamped his mouth shut.

"Oh, so you two do know each other, hm?" Grey

asked, stepping forward, a meaningful grin on his face. "I thought it was Mac's winning personality that had little kids running up and grabbing him."

Knowing he was trapped into an introduction, Mac said grudgingly, "These two are my niece and nephew, Elly and Simon White, and this is their nanny, Paris Barbour."

Paris gave him a quick, frowning glance, then smiled as Grey gave an unexpected bark of laughter directed at Mac, then stepped forward and took her hand. He bent over it and kissed it in a courtly way that was at odds with his sweat-stained appearance. Paris blushed to the roots of her hair.

"A nanny, hm?" Grey asked. "Sounds like a fascinating job. Does the slavedriver here ever give you a night off so you can tell me all about it? Believe me, I've worked with this guy for years and I know how tough he can be. I'd make a really sympathetic audience. How about this Friday night?"

"She has to work," Mac growled. He juggled the kids so he could reach out and pull Paris's hand out of Grey's. "You got carpenter's glue stuck on your fingers?" he asked pointedly, earning a chuckle from Grey and a look from Paris that questioned his sanity.

Grey rocked back on his heels as he grinned. "Just offering to show the lady a good time. I know she hasn't seen one since she's been working for you."

Mac met his amusement with another scowl. "Why don't you go eat your lunch, then finish framing in the windows on the south wall?"

Grey's chuckle turned into a belly laugh. "You betcha, boss." He grinned again, knuckled each of the kids under the chin so they giggled and ducked their heads against Mac's chest. He gave them a warm look. "So these are Sheila's kids, hm?"

"Yes." Mac remembered that Grey had known her in high school.

"Say hi to her when you talk to her," Grey said. With a good-natured wink at Paris, Grey sauntered toward his truck. "Don't forget about my offer, Miss Barbour. I'll call and make the date."

Not likely, Mac thought ferociously, his gaze sliding to Paris's amused face. The blush was fading from her cheeks, but Grey's flirting had left a glow in her eyes Mac had never seen before, not even when he'd kissed her.

Maybe he should kiss her again just to see if he could make her eyes shine like that for him.

And how many ways could a man make a fool of himself in the space of five minutes? he asked himself. So far, he'd racked up any number.

He settled the children more firmly against him and asked, "What are you doing here, Paris? Is something wrong?"

He'd intended to put a little distance between them, but his cold tone had opened a chasm. She lifted that pointed little chin of hers and aimed it directly at him with all the accuracy of a heat-seeking missile.

"You forgot your lunch, so we brought it to you. We packed some for ourselves and we're going to have a picnic on the beach. The kids would like it if you joined us."

In other words, she didn't care if he did or not. Perversely, he decided that was exactly what he wanted to do. What was the point of having a family, even a temporary one, if he couldn't knock off an hour from work and enjoy them? This righteous thought pleased him and he ignored the inner voice that reminded him he'd planned to do his duty in providing for the children and not much else. Knocking off an hour to spend time with them hadn't been included in his plans.

"Nothing would make me happier," he said, enjoying the way she blinked in surprise.

"Oh, all right then," she said, recovering quickly. Her eyes lit with pleasure. "Let's go down to the beach." She held up the items in her arms. "I brought a blanket and your lunch," she added pointedly.

Mac felt his lips twitch. "Thanks. I forgot it."

She lifted one tawny eyebrow at him.

He grinned. Why had he thought he was going to have the last word on the food issue? He'd hardly had the last word on anything since the day she'd walked into his life. Except for that business of her taking the kids into town. He thought she finally understood his feelings about that.

"Is there a shady spot where we can spread the blanket?" she asked.

"I think there's a place under the cliff that's out of the direct sun." Hitching Simon up against his chest and setting Elly on her feet, he turned toward the path that snaked down to the beach. "Let's go."

Paris hung back for a moment as she enjoyed the sight of him carrying Simon and directing Elly's unsure steps. The momentary nervousness she'd felt over showing up at his worksite had faded into annoyance at the pointed way he'd interrupted his friend's mild flirting.

She knew for a fact that he didn't feel anything akin to possessiveness toward her since that would be totally inappropriate, even in light of the kiss they'd shared. Was he afraid that if she met a man who interested her, she'd spend her time with him instead of on the job?

Pretty ironic considering he'd tried to fire her just yesterday.

Paris gave a mental shrug and hurried after him. She'd
already decided that she wasn't going to be able to figure
out the way he thought.

At the bottom of the path, Mac turned right and strode
over the rocky beach, bending his head and listening
intently as Elly chattered. The awkwardness he'd shown
with the children at first was gone. It was touching to
see the careful way he watched over them.

Paris felt warmth rush through her. Could Mac see
how he'd changed? How much the children had
changed? How secure they felt with him? She hoped so.
They needed and deserved to feel secure. The thought
of their security brought Sheila to mind.

As soon as Mac found the place he was looking for,
he set Simon down and they began exploring along the
beach. Paris found a patch of soft sand and spread out
the blanket, then kicked off her sandals and knelt to set
out their lunch. As she worked, she told Mac about
Sheila's call.

"What do you think it means?" she asked, giving him
a curious look.

Mac stood slowly and tucked his hands into his back
pockets as he watched the children step to the edge of
the water. "I don't know," he admitted. "I thought
she'd probably call to check on them, for show if not
out of real concern."

"That was the impression I got," Paris said sadly.
"As if calling to check on her children was something
she'd heard she was supposed to do."

"Yes, that was probably all that was behind her call,
but…" his voice trailed off.

"What?" Paris answered.

"It bothers me that I don't ever remember her acting worried about them," he said. Solemnly, he watched Elly and Simon as they crept close to the waves. Laughing, Elly scooted back, pulling her little brother with her.

Paris felt a spark of happiness that he had admitted his feelings to her. But she also felt an ache of sadness for Mac and his disappointment in his sister. She smiled to herself as he stepped closer to the children, ready to dash over and grab them if they got too close to the water. Perhaps Sheila had never developed the kind of concern she needed to have as a mother, but with a little encouragement and practice, that concern was flourishing in Mac.

"But then, I wasn't around them much," he went on. "I think she didn't want her big brother interfering in her life." He laughed but it held no amusement. "I guess she got enough of that when she was a kid."

"How much older are you than she is?" she asked.

"Ten years. Our parents were already entering middle age when she was born and didn't have the energy to keep up with her, so it fell to me." He shook his head. "I know our parents loved her, but she was too much for them, so she didn't have a very good example of what parents were supposed to do. Maybe that's why she's like she is." He made a disgusted sound low in his throat. "Or maybe she's just selfish and can't make time for them in her life."

He frowned and stared broodingly at the tide that washed in and out, teasing the children. Paris felt tears spurt into her eyes. She lifted her hand and touched his forearm. "*You're* making time for them, Mac. That's what matters right now."

He glanced down at her hand and she felt the muscles

move beneath her palm. His eyes met hers. "Does it? I wonder if I'm doing right by them. After all, I was the only adult role model Sheila really had, and look how she turned out."

Paris dropped her hand and sat back on her heels. If a man was determined to be hard on himself, there wasn't much she could do about it. Mentally, she cast about for a change of subject. "My mother was past forty when I was born and my dad was fifty-one."

Mac took his eyes off the children for a moment and flicked her an interested glance as if he was glad to get his thoughts off his irresponsible sister. "Did you lead them a merry chase?"

"No, I was a quiet, docile little girl."

Mac's dark eyes widened and she saw humor lurking in them. "When did you change?"

Paris swallowed the temptation to tell him it had happened the day she'd met him. "You mean when did I become bossy and nosy?"

He grinned. "Yeah."

"Only recently," she answered. She didn't want to go into the whole story of her marriage and the tremendous changes it had brought in her life, or the way that being around Mac had challenged her to be more forthright and firm in sticking by her beliefs.

Strangely, Mac seemed to understand her reluctance. He stared at her speculatively for a moment before he nodded, one corner of his mouth lifting in a fleeting smile. Turning, he wandered down to the water's edge to be with Elly and Simon.

He helped them remove their shoes so they could splash in the water, and it wasn't long before he'd pulled off his own workboots and tossed his socks aside. He rolled up his pants legs and joined them in a game of tag with the tiny waves that lapped the sand and rocks. He held their hands and lifted them in bouncing steps as the cold water hit their feet. They shrieked in time to the bounces.

Charmed, Paris sat with her hands in her lap and watched the three of them, aware of a sense of peace and rightness that settled inside her. Her thoughts circled back to where they'd been a few minutes ago. Whether he knew it or not, Mac was changing. Even if caring for Elly and Simon was only a temporary arrangement, his life was being permanently altered by them.

She was changing, too, she realized with a feeling of surprise. She didn't have much time to dwell on the unhappiness and occasional bitter thoughts toward people in her past when her mind was full of the concerns of caring for two small children and deciphering the puzzle of Mac Weston. In fact, she felt happy for the first time in more than a year and it was a feeling she savored.

Seeing that Mac and the children were watching something at the edge of the water, she jumped to her feet and hurried to join in the fun.

"What did you find?"

"It's a cwab," Elly said, her eyes shining with discovery as the small crustacean scuttled away across the sand. "But it doesn't look like Unka Mac."

Paris grinned but Mac straightened and gave his niece a puzzled look.

"Did you think it was supposed to look like Uncle Mac?" Paris asked, sneaking a peek at him.

Elly shrugged. "Well, my mommy said that sometimes Unka Mac can be cwabby."

Mac scowled ferociously as Paris hooted with laughter. Seeing his expression, she tried to stifle her humor, but it sparkled in her eyes. "I'm sure your mommy was only joking, Elly."

"Oh no, huh-uh," Elly said, shaking her head vigorously. "She said Unka Mac was bossy and cwabby. That's what she said, huh Simon?" She appealed to her little brother who didn't answer because he was busy trying to follow the crab as it scurried for cover in a pile of seaweed. "Isn't that what Mommy said? But we had to do what he said anyway."

Unable to resist, Paris gave Mac a teasing look as she answered the little girl. "I'm sure your mommy knew what she was talking about, Elly. After all, she's known your Uncle Mac longer than any of us."

Elly nodded and looked up. "Can you swim as good as a cwab, Unka Mac?"

"Oh, I can swim better," he answered, but his eyes, gleaming dangerously, were fixed on Paris. "I wonder how well Paris can swim, though," he said, taking a gliding stride forward. "I'm thinking maybe we should find out."

"What?" Paris stepped back in alarm.

"I know you grew up in the desert, but surely they have swimming pools there. I'll bet you know how to swim."

"Uh, no," she said, glancing behind her to see if she had a clear route of escape. "Can't swim a stroke. And uh, no swimming pools in Hadley."

Mac lifted a skeptical brow at the obvious lie.

"Only irrigation ditches," Paris said. "And it's hard to swim in irrigation ditches."

"Is it now?" he asked softly, his long legs taking one quick step toward her. "So you're saying that since you can't swim, maybe I shouldn't throw you in the Pacific Ocean?"

She nodded her head vigorously as she lifted her skirt around her knees and danced back several more steps. "That's exactly what I'm saying."

"I don't think I agree with you. I think I need to do exactly that right now."

Seeing the purpose in his eyes, Paris whirled around, broke and ran. Behind her, she felt something pluck at her shirt and knew Mac had made a grab for her. She put on more speed, but aware that she couldn't get too far away from the children who were still at the water's edge, she knew she would have to double back pretty soon. The question was, how was she going to manage that with Mr. Quick Hands behind her?

Thinking fast, she jumped to the right, stopped abruptly, then whirled around and started to dash back in the other direction. Mac barreled past her, but stopped with a roar when he saw that she'd tricked him. Laughing, Paris ran harder.

As she looked ahead, she saw that she needn't have worried about the children. Elly was jumping up and down and shrieking as the two adults chased down the beach. Taking his cue from his sister, Simon was trying to hop in place in imitation of her. He was bottom-heavy though, and could only manage to get a few millimeters of lift. Still, he shouted with laughter, too. As she dashed past, Paris made a funny, desperate face at them, making them laugh all the harder.

Again, she felt something fan across her back and she tried to run faster, but it was hard to do since most of her breath was taken up with laughter. Mac's hand settled on her shoulder and gripped hard enough to stop her and spin her around to face him.

"A...crab, hm?" he asked on puffs of breath. "Paris,

you need to learn that it's not a good idea to insult your employer," he reminded her.

"I know. He might try to fire me," she teased.

"He might succeed."

She shook her head. "Nah. He usually listens to reason after a while. Besides, I've got an advantage."

When her hair shifted across his hand, Mac grasped a gentle handful of it and used it to hold her so that her eyes met his. His gaze dropped to her lips, then came back to her eyes. "And what would that be?"

Her breath was settling down, but her heart was a quick, light patter in her throat. She loved this side of him, loved to see the way he must once have been before circumstances had made life hard for him. Laughing up at him, she tilted her head. "Them," she said just as Elly and Simon careened into the backs of his legs, sending him stumbling forward. His arms wrapped around her to steady himself and Paris's hands shot up to grasp him around the waist.

With a wicked grin, he said, "I guess you *do* have the advantage." His lips swept down to graze hers in a tingling touch that left her wanting more. He pulled away and bent to scoop up the children.

"Unka Mac, why were you chasing Pris?" Elly wanted to know.

His eyes still on Paris's, Mac answered. "Because she was trying to get away."

Elly wiggled around so that she could put her arms around the necks of both adults. "We don't want her to get away."

"No, we don't," he agreed.

Warmth radiated through Paris, bringing with it a surge of incredible joy at being here with these children and this man. This was what she'd always wanted, what she'd hoped for with Keith and never had.

"Now kiss me and Simon," Elly demanded. She turned her head rapidly from one to the other of them so that her bright red hair flashed in the sunlight.

"Yes, ma'am," Paris said, dutifully giving each child a smacking kiss on the cheek, which Mac imitated, making them giggle.

Mac gave his niece a considering look. "Do you think I ought to kiss Paris, too?"

Paris stared, remembering the kiss they'd shared in his kitchen. He wasn't going to do that here, was he? Right in front of the children?

"No," Elly said.

"No," Simon echoed, though Paris doubted he really understood what was going on.

"Are you *sure* I shouldn't kiss Paris?" Mac asked Elly, but his eyes were on Paris and the wariness growing there. Her heartbeat, which had just begun to settle down, speeded up again. Tension curled through her and she could see an answering spurt of need in Mac's eyes.

"Nuh-uh," Elly answered.

"Why not?" Mac's expression seemed to be questioning her. *Will you?* he seemed to ask.

Paris's lips trembled open. She wanted to say yes, but the word clogged in her throat.

"'Cause it takes too long. I saw it on TV. Big people just kiss and kiss and kiss and me and Simon would have to wait and wait and wait," Elly answered in a long-suffering tone.

The adults burst out laughing, breaking the tension between them.

"I thought you were monitoring what they've been watching on television," Mac said.

Paris held up her hands. "Hey, I do. She probably saw an advertisement for mouthwash."

"A likely story," he muttered, but she saw laughter in his eyes.

Paris reached out to take Simon from Mac's arms, then they turned and began walking back to their waiting picnic.

"This is fun," Elly declared.

Mac looked over at Paris, who met his look with a warm smile. "Yes, it is," he said.

"We need more picnics," the little girl went on, then gave her uncle a sly look. "We could have a picnic at the park."

He gave the little girl a sharp glance, then looked back at Paris, who shrugged innocently.

"Maybe we'll have to do that," he conceded. "But only if I come with you."

Elly sighed and laid her head on his shoulder. "That's what I've always wanted. For you to be with me."

Me too, Paris thought as they strolled down the rocky beach. In spite of the warm sun, she shivered at the truth in that statement. She wanted Mac to be with her, to *be* hers.

CHAPTER EIGHT

To Paris's surprise, Grey Taggart called her that very night and asked her out.

"There's a great country and western club in Alban," he said. "It's called The Lucky Spur. Do you know how to line dance?"

Paris's stunned gaze flew across the kitchen to where Mac sat watching Elly color a picture for him. So far, it consisted mostly of lines and scribbles, but he'd told her she had great promise as an architect, then had to explain what that was in terms a four-year-old would understand. He was still at it.

"Well, uh, Grey, it's very nice of you to ask me…um, to The Lucky Spur…." she stammered. "But I'm afraid I don't know how to line dance."

"Hey, that's okay," he answered breezily. "You can learn."

Across the room, she saw Mac's head come up and his attention snap to her face which experienced a ridiculous tendency to blush bright red. She wound the phone cord around her fingers even as she wondered why she was so nervous.

"Fine. How about Friday night?" he asked eagerly.

"This Friday?"

"You don't have other plans, do you?"

"Well, no, but I'll have to work, I'm sure, and…"

"No, you don't," Mac interrupted. He stood suddenly, strode across the kitchen and took the receiver from her hand. "Grey?" He spoke into the phone, but his eyes were on her. "She'll be glad to go. It's her night off." He paused to listen.

Paris made a grab for the phone, but he held her off. She clapped her hands onto her hips and stared at him as surprise and embarrassment faded from her face to be replaced by annoyance.

"Sure, buddy," he said. "I'll tell her. See you tomorrow." He tossed the receiver back onto its cradle and said, "He'll pick you up at seven. Wear your dancing shoes."

He turned his back and stalked to the table while Paris fought the urge to snatch up a rolling pin and chase him with it.

"Oh, Mr. Weston?" she said in her sweetest tone of voice.

He turned around, his eyes wary. She knew he'd never heard that tone from her and expected something to drop on his head. Smart man.

"Yes?"

She walked over to stand close enough to look directly into his face. "Exactly when did Friday night become my night off?"

Mac lifted a shoulder in a shrug, but his dark eyes were cautious. "I realized we never made arrangements for you to have time off. You're not a prisoner here. You're an employee."

Unaccountably, that hurt. After the fun they'd had that day, the closeness they'd experienced, she had thought there was more between them than a boss and hired help relationship.

Clearly, she'd been wrong.

She had more to say to him, but aware of Elly's big eyes on them, and remembering how she'd reacted the last time the two of them got into an argument, Paris

smiled at him with enough coolness to have frost bloom-
ing on his eyebrows and turned back to the dinner preparations. As soon as the children were in bed, though,
she decided, vigorously chopping onions, the hired help
and Mr. High-handed Weston were going to have a talk.

It seemed to take forever to get Elly and Simon settled
into bed that night. They were overstimulated from the
picnic that day and from the novelty of having their uncle's undivided attention all evening. Paris called herself
a hypocrite because she'd wanted him to pay attention
to the children. Now, though, she suspected his atten-
tiveness had been prompted by his desire to avoid her.
After all, did he have to read them *seven* bedtime stories? She usually only read one or two because she didn't
want them to get into the habit of delaying bedtime.

It was evident that they'd learned those delaying tac-
tics from a very near relative. When he finished the sev-
enth book, Mac snapped it shut, gave both children a
quick kiss, and hustled from the room.

Paris gave his disappearing back a disgruntled look as
she tucked Elly in and spread a loose blanket over Simon
who would kick it off within seconds, anyway, then hurried from their room in time to see Mac's bedroom door
closing quietly. She scrambled down the hall and
grabbed the edge of the door, which almost pinched her
fingers.

Wincing, she said, "I'd like to talk to you, Mac."

"Oh?" He gave her an innocent look. "About
what?"

She pushed the door wider and pursued him into the
room. "About you making dates for me with Grey
Taggart."

"Don't you like Grey?" he asked, looking surprised—or as surprised as a sneak could look, she thought.

"I don't *know* Grey."

"Oh, well," Mac said with a dismissive wave of his hand. "That's what dates are for, though, right? You can get to know him, but if you need a recommendation, I've known him all his life and I can tell you he's a nice enough guy, if you like the type."

Knowing she was going to hate herself for allowing this sidetrack into a ridiculous conversation, Paris tilted her chin defiantly, crossed her arms over her chest, and asked, "What type would that be?"

"Laid-back. Not interested in commitment. Grey likes women, but his girlfriend, Monica Barris, dumped him last month because he wasn't interested in marriage." He held up his hands.

Paris felt her back teeth begin to grind together. "Well, isn't that a coincidence? That makes two of us. For your information, though, I don't date men I just met."

"What kind of men do you date?" he asked, looking at her curiously.

None. She hadn't been out with anyone except Keith, hadn't had the slightest interest in anyone since his death—until she'd met Mac.

When she didn't answer, Mac went on, "Go out with Grey. You'll have fun. He's always good for a laugh."

"Unlike some people I could name," she muttered, staring at him in frustration.

"What?"

"Never mind," she sighed, exasperated. "Let's get back to the point."

"Which is?"

"I don't need you to make dates for me. I can make my own dates."

"With who? Floyd and Benny Lyte? They're the only other men you've met since you've been in Cliffside."

"Well, then I don't want a date with *anyone*," she said, throwing her arms wide.

"How are you ever going to find another husband if you don't date?" Mac asked.

Paris gaped at him. Where had *that* come from? "Weren't you listening? I said I'm not interested in marriage." Maybe that wasn't strictly true, but she was annoyed with him. "When did I ever indicate I'm interested in another husband?"

"You need one," he said in that same oh-so-sure-of-himself tone. "You're good with kids. You'd make a good mom."

Stunned, Paris couldn't think of a thing to say. Her mouth opened and closed a couple of times and finally all she could do was make a tiny squeak of rage. She'd thought he saw her as something other than a caretaker of children, but she'd certainly been wrong!

"Give Grey a chance," Mac said, blithely ignoring her fury. "You'll like him. He's athletic, plays on the local softball team. Maybe you can go some night and watch him flex his muscles."

"I don't care if he's an Olympic contender, I don't want to..." Her voice trailed off as an idea occurred to her. Mac never did anything without a reason so there had to be a good one for this sudden urge to find her a date. Could it be that he wanted her out of the house so he could have the kids to himself? No, he was growing closer to them, but he didn't want to do her job for her. Maybe he just didn't want *her* around so much because he was regretting his playfulness on the beach that day and in spite of his words to the contrary, he was no longer seeing her as the hired hand. She gave him a speculative look. Maybe. Maybe not.

When she didn't finish her thought, Mac took her arm and propelled her out the door. ''Don't forget. Seven o'clock Friday night. He'll be here with bells on.'' Ushering Paris out into the hall, he stepped back inside and closed the door in her annoyed face.

It took several seconds for Paris to gather her wits. When she did, she gave his bedroom door a resounding kick, then limped down the hall to her own room. There was no use trying to make sense of this. The man was plainly trying to push her away. Fine. She'd go out with Grey and have a wonderful time.

What had he been thinking? Mac wondered as he watched the lights of Grey's car disappear up the driveway. He hadn't wanted her to go out with Grey. Grey was okay. Everyone liked him. Everything Mac had told Paris was true: Grey was laid-back, fun, athletic. Available.

Too available, Mac thought scowling as he prowled to the next window, searching for a last glimpse of the lights.

Grey had shown up driving the Camaro he hardly ever took out of his garage, his boots shining like a couple of rotating airport beacons, hair slicked down, wearing enough cologne to send Paris into an allergy attack—if she had allergies. And if she didn't have them, she would before the night was over.

The *night?* She'd darned well better be back here before the night was too old. By ten o'clock at the latest, or Mac vowed he'd go find her. A woman responsible for two small children shouldn't be out too late. She needed her rest to deal with them.

"Oh, hell," he muttered, then looked around quickly to see if Simon had heard him. In the last two days, the little boy had begun dogging his steps and repeating everything he said, including a number of words that had Paris threatening to wash Mac's mouth out with soap. Relieved, he saw that the children were engrossed in their books and toys which were spread all over the living room floor and hadn't heard his lapse.

Mac had no one but himself to blame for this. The minute he'd heard her on the phone with Grey he'd been hit with a wave of jealousy that felt like a left hook to the gut. Paradoxically, it had made him react exactly the opposite way of what he should have. He'd taken it on himself to make a date for her with Grey. She'd been justifiably furious and had hardly spoken to him since except to ask him to pass the salt at dinner or wipe Simon's hands before he got down from the table.

Then tonight, when she'd walked out of her bedroom, his tongue had stuck itself to the roof of his mouth as if he'd swallowed a slug of carpenter's glue.

She hadn't been wearing her usual jeans or loose flowing skirt. Oh, no. In honor of the occasion, she'd donned a black dress with a short full skirt and a silver belt that had shown off a waist tinier than he'd suspected it was. She'd swayed down the hall on three-inch heels, her hair a mass of gold-shot curls around her shoulders and presented herself for Elly's inspection. His traitorous little niece had said she was the most beautiful nanny in the world. In fact, the most beautiful *anything* in the world.

Unfortunately, he couldn't disagree with that assessment and Grey's eyes had nearly popped out of his head when Paris had opened the door for him.

Grumpily, Mac prowled the living room, checking all the windows again just in case there was one last glimpse of them, and stopping to read a few books to Elly and Simon before he put them to bed. When they were asleep, he went back to prowling the house from the kitchen window to the living room and back to the kitchen with its view of the driveway.

He'd spent way too much time thinking about Paris since he'd chased her up the beach. It shook him right down to his workboots to realize how important she had become to him.

He needed distance from her, he thought, scowling at the empty driveway. Sure the kids adored her, and his house had never felt more warm, inviting, and comfortable as it had since she'd been there, nor had he ever eaten so well.

Still, he needed to make sure it was well understood that she was an employee, that her private life was her own and of no concern to him, that the information he'd given her about Grey simply meant he was concerned for an employee.

That decided, he looked at the clock and forgot all about the lecture he'd given himself.

Eight o'clock. What were they doing? And what kind of place was The Lucky Spur, anyway? He'd never been there. His fiancée, Judith, wouldn't have been caught dead in a country and western bar.

Were the lights too low? The drinks too strong? Good-natured Grey too appealing to a lonely widow? Mac tortured himself with the images those thoughts conjured up.

He roamed back to the living room and stood with his hands in his back pockets, noticing, not for the first time lately that his jeans didn't ride down his hips anymore.

He'd gained nearly ten pounds since Paris had been working for him. True, he'd had his doubts at first, but she'd worked out exactly as she'd promised she would. She was a fine cook and a conscientious nanny.

But was he being a conscientious boss? Mac straightened and stared out at the darkness. What kind of man, what kind of boss, made a date for his employee without even knowing the setup she was going to get herself into? Sure, he knew Grey and he was a good guy even if he did have a lazy attitude toward life. What about the other men at that Lucky Spur place. Exactly how lucky did the men in that bar expect to get, anyway? When they saw Paris sashay inside wearing that short black dress, were they going to react like they'd hit some kind of communal lottery?

Mac felt queasy at the thought of the uncomfortable situation he'd manipulated Paris into. He ought to be horsewhipped, he thought in disgust.

Making a rapid decision, he stalked to the kitchen and grabbed the phone. Punching out a number, he barked, "Becky, I need a favor."

The country band was so loud, Paris could feel it pounding in her chest.

"This is great, isn't it?" Grey asked, leaning close as he showed her the next step in the dance he was trying to teach her.

Slide, step, side step, back. No, that wasn't right, she thought in confusion as she bounced off a mountain of a man dancing behind her. Mumbling an apology, she moved away and immediately stepped on the foot of a woman near her. It would help if the place wasn't so crowded, and if she could breathe, but between the press of people in the room and the cloud of cologne hanging foglike around Grey, there wasn't much oxygen to be had.

"Paris? This is great, huh?" he repeated.

"Uh, yeah," she said, managing a smile that was only the tiniest bit less wobbly than her feet in these wicked high heels.

Grey took her arm, put his hand around her waist, and swung her into the next step at warp speed. Paris clung to him as she waited for her head to catch up with the rest of her body and snap back into place.

What had she been thinking, anyway? Defiantly, she'd worn a dress guaranteed to knock a man's eyes out, but it had been Mac's eyes she'd pictured rolling on the floor, not Grey's. Mac was the one she'd wanted to impress with her leg-enhancing three-inch heels, not Grey.

She should have worn boots and jeans like every other woman in this place. She'd grown up around country and western bars. There were no other kind in Hadley. She knew what she should have worn, but she'd succumbed to annoyance and vanity, wanting to punish Mac for fixing her up on this unwanted date. However, Mac couldn't have cared less. The indifference in his expression when she'd emerged from her room had told her that.

And what had her vanity gained her? Wobbly ankles and arches screaming for relief.

Grey gave her a good-natured grin and she smiled back. Really, he was a nice guy, and lots of fun. It wasn't his fault she'd been foolish in her choice of footwear.

"You're catching on just great," he complimented her even though she'd stepped on his feet six times in as many minutes. "Next time we go out you'll know just what to do."

Yes, she thought. *Stay home and read a good book.*

She couldn't hurt his feelings, though, so as the music stopped, she said, "I sure will, Grey. Thanks for all your patience with me."

"Hey, it's okay. Just trying to show a lady a good time."

Paris had to admire the way he kept from limping on the way back to their table. When they sat down, he saw that his beer was warm and Paris's cola had been watered down with melting ice cubes, so he headed for the bar for another round of drinks.

Paris took advantage of his absence to rub her forehead and wonder why she hadn't packed some aspirin in her tiny purse.

"Having fun yet?" a voice asked near her left ear.

With a startled squeak, she turned to see her boss looming over her. "Mac? What are you doing here?" She glanced around quickly. "Where are the kids?"

"Calm down," he said, slipping into the seat beside her. "I didn't leave them alone. Becky's baby-sitting. I thought I'd better come and see how everything's going since I was the one who got you into this date." He glanced around. "So, how *is* it going?"

Paris stared at him, and then glared, her green-gold eyes narrowing in concentration. "You're checking up on me? Exactly what is it you think I'm going to do? Embarrass you in some way?"

His eyes snapped to her. "Hey, no, of course not. I'm just here to make sure Grey's treating you right." He turned his attention to the dance floor. "And, uh, to see if you like line dancing."

Her jaw dropped. "To see if I like *line dancing?*"

Mac answered with a feeble wave of his hand. "Well, you know how it is. I feel responsible, and…" His voice trailed off and he stared at the dancers as if he'd never seen anything so fascinating.

Paris stared at *him*. He'd called Becky to baby-sit, showered, brushed his hair, shaved, splashed himself with that mouth-watering aftershave of his, dressed in clean jeans and a shirt she'd ironed last Tuesday, and—Paris leaned over to peek under the table—shined his boots for the sole purpose of coming to see if she liked line dancing?

No way. No way at all.

For the first time since Grey had called and Mac had set her up on this date, joy bubbled through her. She burst out laughing.

"That's the lamest excuse I've ever heard in my life, Mackenzie Weston. Why are you really here?" She thought she knew, but she wanted to hear him say it.

He gave her a disgruntled look. "I told you, I wanted to see if…"

"Can it, Mac," she said, grinning. "Tell me why you're really here."

He looked at her, then away, then back again. His feet shuffled under the table as he stood and pulled her to her feet. "Let's dance."

She let him tug her out of her chair, but she didn't move from the side of the table. Instead, she placed one hand on her hip and the other squarely in the middle of his chest.

"Uh-uh. Not until you tell me why you're here." Oh, she was enjoying this.

He examined the row of branding irons that were set in a zigzag pattern around the top of the wall. Finally, his gaze met hers.

"I was jealous, okay?" he said in a low, furious tone, shooting his hand up to trap hers in place against his chest. "I didn't want you dancing with anyone else. Not on those legs."

She snickered. "I left my spare legs in my other pair of pantyhose."

He ignored that bit of silliness as he went on. "And especially not in that dress."

"I guess I could dance without it," she said impishly, letting him draw her to him and following his lead into the slow dance that had just begun.

"Not even in your dreams, girl," he muttered into her ear as he pulled her close.

Happiness overwhelmed her and she felt inexplicable tears spurt into her eyes. He was jealous. She couldn't believe it. The man who hadn't even wanted her around, who didn't think she could take care of his niece and nephew, was nothing but a misplaced country club socialite, was jealous that she was out with another man. She'd never considered jealousy to be an attractive quality in a man, but in one like Mac, who didn't show his feelings easily, it was flattering. More than flattering. His discomfort with the knowledge of it touched her deeply.

So deeply in fact, that as she moved around the crowded dance floor in his arms, her cheek against the strength of his chest, she could finally acknowledge something that had been growing in her for days now. She was in love with him.

She loved Mac Weston even when she wanted to thump him on the forehead for his stubbornness. Even when she couldn't understand him and the reasons he did what he did, she loved him.

Ever since the day she had come to his home, she had admired his integrity for taking in two small children, for working so hard to salvage his reputation, to start his life over again. That admiration had grown into love that

filled her with delight, joy, and fright. She had only ever
loved one other man and he had chosen to grieve himself
to death over his failures rather than to fight to make
himself into a success like Mac had done.

On the heels of the happiness she felt knowing she
loved him, Paris also felt a hint of sadness. In spite of
all she had tried to do, she felt as if she had failed Keith.
She didn't want to fail Mac. Besides, she doubted that
he would welcome a declaration of her love. To him, it
would be another responsibility to carry, maybe even a
burden.

Drawing in a wobbly breath, she vowed that she
would keep it a secret at least for now.

"Hey, something wrong?" he asked, holding her
away to look down at her.

"No," she said, her lips springing into a bright smile.
"Everything's fine. Now. I have a question, though."

"What's that?"

She nodded toward the bar. "See that guy in the spiffy
green cowboy shirt?"

"You mean the one with the cloud of cologne hanging
around him like a San Francisco June fog? What about
him?"

"He thinks he's my date tonight."

"No kidding? I guess I'll have to set him straight
about that." Mac slipped his arms around her and hers
slid up around his neck.

"Mac, I'm not the kind of girl who goes out with one
man and comes home with another," she said seriously.

"Even if the other man lives in the same house with
you?"

"That's right."

"How do you know you're not that kind of girl?
You've never done this before."

"I just know." She glanced back at Grey who had finally managed to get their drinks and was maneuvering his way back to their table.

Mac looked at Grey, then down at her. "Okay, he takes you home, but I meet you at the door." With that, he released her and melted into the crowd.

Paris blinked, unable to believe how quickly he'd disappeared, then turned and squeezed her way through the press of bodies.

"Oh, there you are," Grey said, setting down their drinks and pulling out her chair for her. "Drink up, then let's dance some more. You're really catching on," he said enthusiastically. Paris gave him a wavering smile. She didn't want to dance anymore. She wanted to go home to Mac.

Grey gave her a slow grin. "Was that Mac I saw in here a minute ago?"

Dismayed, Paris looked at him. She didn't want to hurt his feelings, but she said, "Yes."

"He came to check on you, did he?"

"Yes." What else could she say?

Grey chuckled into his drink. "I thought he was showing a little more interest than he normally would in an employee." He shrugged. "After all, I've worked for him off and on for years and he's never seemed to care where *I* went dancing on Friday night."

Paris smiled in response, but she wondered exactly where Grey was going with this.

Grey leaned closer. "Seriously," he said. "Mac's a good guy, but he's too hard on himself, too willing to take on responsibility that's not his, like Sheila's kids, and…well, other things." Sitting back, Grey sipped his drink.

"What things, Grey? You mean the school building that collapsed?"

"Yeah, and all the fallout from that. There's more, but he'll have to tell you about it himself." Grey grinned suddenly. "Let's dance. I have the feeling this is the only time I'm ever going to be able to take you out, so I'd better make the most of it. I'm guessing that if Mac's coming here to check on you, he's not going to let you out of his sight again."

Paris laughed, hoping it was true, as she took Grey's hand and went with him back to the dance floor.

After several more dances, they started back to Mac's house. Paris could barely contain her excitement because she knew Mac would be waiting for her. Grey walked her to the door, gave her a good-night hug, and said he wished they could go dancing again, but he didn't want Mac to push him off a roof beam.

"I'd hate to see that happen," Paris said, standing on tiptoe to give him a soft kiss on the cheek. With a cocky grin, Grey left, whistling his way up the front walk and Paris reached for the doorknob.

Before she could even give it a twist, the door opened, a hand reached out to clasp her around the waist, and she was reeled inside to Mac's waiting arms.

His mouth came down on hers. "I thought he'd never leave," he murmured against her lips.

"He was only here for ten seconds," she protested, sliding her arms around him and meeting his lips with hers.

"It was nine seconds too long," Mac answered, closing his lips over hers so that all thought was blocked out. "Long enough for you to kiss him."

"It was a thank-you," she answered breathlessly. "For a nice evening."

"Well, you're home now," he growled. "And the best part of the evening is before us."

Mac kissed her as if he were a starving man, and Paris met his passion with her own. He brought her up on her toes so that he could reach her more easily. His lips devoured hers, then pulled away to drop kisses on her cheeks, her jaw, her eyelids.

"I thought I'd go crazy tonight when you left with him," he admitted between kisses.

"I didn't want to go with him. I wanted it to be you."

"Nah, I can't line dance."

Laughing softly, Paris caught his face between her hands, rubbing her palms over his smooth cheeks, blessing him for shaving so meticulously. His mouth was firm, delicious, and so welcome. He filled up the loneliness that had plagued her since long before Keith's death. She loved him and it seemed as if the words to tell him so trembled on her lips in spite of her determination to keep the secret.

Paris pressed against Mac, but still felt as if she couldn't get close enough. She kicked off her high heels and stood on top of his boots.

His quiet chuckle cut off as he groaned, "We could sit down and do this."

"You don't have a couch," she pointed out.

"No, but I've got a bed."

Paris went very still. Longing for him almost sent her to her knees. She loved him. It filled her, seemed to ooze out through her very pores, but she couldn't do as he was suggesting, not unless he loved her, too.

"I can't, Mac," she said, pulling away and searching his face.

He hooked his hands together behind her waist. "You

can't tell me you don't want me as much as I want you. I won't believe you."

She swallowed hard. "Wanting and having are two different things, Mac."

"And I can't have you?" he asked harshly.

Paris placed her hand on his cheek. "Look at it both ways. I can't have you, either. The time isn't right."

"What could be more right than this?" he asked, pulling her to him so that she could feel the strength of his need for her. That almost finished her right there. She needed him in exactly the same way.

"Mac, please," she said. "This…this would complicate things so badly, don't you see that?" She prayed that he would understand, because she couldn't explain any more fully than that. If she made love with him and there was no commitment between them, she would be devastated and her loneliness would be even worse.

Mac grasped her waist as if he couldn't let her go, then he pulled her forward and ground his forehead against hers. "This is murder," he complained, then his arms loosened and his hands slid up to cup her shoulders. They tightened there for a moment, and then slipped down her arms to grasp her hands loosely in his. "I know you're not a tease," he said. "You're an honest woman and you don't have a coy bone in your body, so I think there must be more going on here than I know about. Are you still in love with your husband?"

Paris blinked. She hadn't expected that but the question somehow gave her a spark of hope.

"I'll always love him," she answered honestly. "He was important to me and in many ways he helped make me the person I am today, but I didn't die with him." She gave a short laugh. "It took me a long time to come back to life, but I didn't die with him."

She wanted to tell Mac that she'd begun to come back to life the day he'd hired her, but the words clotted together in her throat. Such an admission might spur him to more of those passionate kisses and she wasn't sure she could withstand them. Or him.

Mac was silent for a long time, his dark eyes roaming her features as if he was memorizing them. "All right," he finally said, slowly, reluctantly. "I'm not going to push you into this." A sexy smile broke over his face. "But you know where to find me if you want me."

Oh, she wanted him all right. There was no doubt of that. "Yes, Mac," she answered in a small voice. "I do."

With one last kiss, he set her away from him and turned to leave the room. As she watched him go, Paris felt a wave of anticipation mixed with sadness that she couldn't quite define.

Her life had begun to change the moment Mac had opened his front door to her. Caring for Elly and Simon, learning to love them, and eventually, their uncle had completed her transformation, and for better or worse, she was altered forever.

She was ready to move past the bitterness that had been her constant companion for so long and a large share of the credit for that went to Mac.

A part of her heart would always belong to him. The question, though, was whether or not he would want it.

CHAPTER NINE

"I DON'T know that this is such a good idea," Mac said, stopping his truck in the small parking lot and staring ahead at the swing sets and jungle gyms.

"Why not?" Paris asked.

Mac leaned over the steering wheel and rested his hands on the top. Slowly, he ran the edge of his thumb along his chin. "Something could happen."

"What could happen?" Paris looked around at the quiet park, seeing more people than she and the children had seen on their previous visit, but still not too many.

There were a few families with small children and an old man sat on a bench near the children's play area. His hat was pulled low over his eyes and his hand moved slowly in and out of a paper sack as he tossed bits of bread and nuts on the ground for the squirrels. A large black Labrador retriever lay at his feet, hungry eyes fixed on the darting squirrels that were benefiting from his master's generosity. He whined each time one of the squirrels drew near, but he didn't chase them.

Several older children played on the jungle gym. A couple of young mothers sat nearby, chatting while they kept an eye on their frolicking youngsters.

"I just don't like surprises," Mac said.

Paris, on the other hand, didn't mind them at all. She had thought there would be tension between them after their ardent kisses of last night and the way she'd had to pull away from him. To her relief, though, Mac was treating her with warmth and tenderness that delighted

140

her even as it puzzled her. Except for the past few days when he'd been playing with Elly and Simon, she'd never seen this gentle side of him before. It made her love him all the more.

She smiled to herself, thinking of all those days ago when she had come to Mac and the children and he'd been so awkward with them.

Now she turned to him with a teasing smile. "Well, you don't have to look as if those are child-eating dinosaurs ready to devour Elly and Simon on sight. Besides, as Elly has reminded you twelve times this morning, you promised to take them to the park."

"You're telling me," he muttered. "My ears are still ringing from all those reminders."

And so here they were, the two adults in the front seat of the truck, "just like a mommy and daddy," Elly had said, and the two children in the smaller second seat of the double cab pickup.

Paris started to answer him, but the children began bouncing in their seats and demanding to be freed.

After a few more seconds of hesitation and another sweeping look around the park, he stepped out and did as they asked. Once she was out of the vehicle, Elly streaked for the swings while Simon steadily plodded along behind, falling once in the soft sand beneath the jungle gym. He pushed himself to his feet and continued, his attention fixed on his goal.

Paris saw the elderly man on the bench stop his listless squirrel feeding and focus on the toddler. He then turned and gave Paris a frowning look as if disapproving that she'd brought children to the park.

Paris looked askance at him, wondering why the man was there at all if he didn't like children. She hurried up to Simon who had rocked to a stop when the black dog raised his head. He crowded up against Paris who took his hand and guided him past Elly's flailing feet and onto a swing with a safety harness.

As she pushed the toddler, Elly struggled to get her swing aloft, insisting that she didn't want help when Paris offered.

Knowing the little girl would probably accept help from her adored uncle, Paris glanced over her shoulder to call out to him. She was surprised to see him, face set in stern lines, hike past the old man who regarded Mac with a malevolent frown. Paris gave the man a nervous look. She hadn't heard about any oddballs hanging around the park, but then, she didn't know much about anyone around here.

On the other hand, maybe the man wasn't an oddball, but instead was one of Mac's enemies.

As she watched, the man got unsteadily to his feet, muttered something unintelligible, and stalked away, pulling the dog's leash so he would come along, too.

His face set, eyes straight ahead, Mac strolled over and gave Elly's swing a shove that had her shrieking with laughter at how high she flew. Paris was dying to ask him about the man, but his closed expression told her he wouldn't welcome questions—not that that was news, she thought wearily, turning her attention back to the children. She experienced a moment of worry at the height Elly's swing reached on each upward motion, but then felt reassured when she saw how carefully Mac was watching his niece.

He glanced over at Paris and she saw the darkness in his expression lift for a moment as he smiled. With a start, Paris realized that he'd known what she was thinking. She smiled back as warmth and buoyant joy flooded through her.

She had seen him smile more in the past two days than she had in all the days since she'd come to live in his house. It thrilled her to know it was brought about by his growing closeness to his niece and nephew and that she had helped foster that closeness.

They spent an hour at the park, following the children from the swings to the slides, to the jungle gym, with frequent stops at the drinking fountain. When Elly and Simon finally settled into the sandbox, Paris and Mac sat on the bench of a nearby picnic table. Mac leaned back with his elbows on the tabletop and stretched his legs out in the most relaxed pose Paris had ever seen him assume.

In fact, despite the ongoing discussion they'd been having about this promised visit to the park and his momentary tension at seeing the man on the bench, she had gradually seen an easing of the strain in him. The playful side of he'd shown on the beach, and again last night, had delighted her and she was eager to see it again. She knew it was a measure of her love for him that she spent so much time thinking about him, his moods, what made him happy or sad. She was hopelessly besotted.

Smiling, she turned to him and held out her hands expansively. "See, now this isn't so bad, is it? You're having a relaxing day, the kids are happy…"

"You got me here so you can stop nagging me now," he finished for her in a dry tone of voice. He rubbed his chin thoughtfully. "Now I know where Elly learned that."

She smirked at him, then lifted her chin, tossed back her tawny curls, and gave him a superior look. "I wasn't nagging. I was simply giving you a forceful suggestion."

"Over and over and over again."

Her eyes danced. "I was afraid you hadn't heard me the first..."

"Few hundred times."

She wrinkled her nose at the way he was finishing her sentences for her. "However, that's not nagging," she responded firmly.

"What is it then?"

"Reinforcement of a previously stated...option."

Mac snorted with laughter and settled back once again to watch the children, a smile softening the usually firm line of his lips. She hoped Mac felt that the children filled a void in his life the way they filled one in hers. He filled a big empty space in her life, too, but that was her secret for now.

The children's contented acceptance of their situation was a lesson to Paris. Although she knew Elly longed for her mother, she didn't ask for her quite as frequently as before. Perhaps, Paris thought, the little girl was simply waiting to see when her mother would come to get her.

Paris watched Elly, her small pink tongue poking out of the side of her mouth as she concentrated on forming damp sand into an artistic mound. "Unka Mac," she asked, looking up suddenly. "Is this the way a car...a carchitect would make a castle?"

With a smile, he assured her that it was exactly as a "carchitect" would build it.

Paris found it amazing that this four-year-old could be tranquil in the face of the changes that had taken place in her life even though her mother had virtually abandoned her, running off to find adventure when the greatest adventure of her life could have been found in raising these two sweet children.

Paris knew she couldn't be judgmental toward Sheila,

though. She, herself, had been alterna[...] furiated, and overwhelmed by the ch[...] stances in her own life.

And what about Mac, she asked h[...] on him. How was he dealing with [...] his life had taken? Was he as ready as she w[...] the past behind and build a future? She wished she [...] the nerve to ask that question.

"Is something wrong?" Mac asked, looking at her with puzzlement.

Heat rushed into her face when she realized how long she'd been staring at him. "No, no. I think I'll…go see if Simon needs a diaper change."

He raised an eyebrow at that excuse. After all, who would be crazy enough to seek out a wet diaper? Paris stood and hurried over to Simon who tried to wiggle out of her arms when she picked him up. He didn't appreciate having his play interrupted. Paris decided the state of his diaper could wait a while.

Turning back to the bench, she saw that Mac was on his feet facing the man who had pointedly stalked away earlier. He was talking in a low, rapid voice. The rigid set of Mac's shoulders and the way his hands were fisted at his sides told her this wasn't a pleasant conversation.

Recalling that she was the nanny and not a self-appointed referee, she was hesitant to approach the two men. However, when Mac's fist raised up and he poked a finger an inch from the other man's nose, she darted forward. She had no idea what she planned to do.

"The children are tired, Mr. Weston," she blurted, trying to sound as nanny-like as possible. "If you're ready, I think we'd better get them home."

Both men turned to her with expressions that asked who she was and what she was doing there. Mac's dark

rled with enough anger to make her step back
tch her breath, though she knew it wasn't directed
r. It took several seconds before he seemed to rec-
nize her and some of the fury began to fade. The
serenity that he had been experiencing moments before
had vanished. Paris's heart sank when she saw the old
wariness return to him.

The other man was breathing hard and made her think
of a steam engine that had built up in force until it was
ready to explode. He gave her a ferocious glare. "Hiding
behind a woman's skirts now, Weston?" he asked.

Mac's expression hardened even more. "Burt," he
said in an even tone. "Stop it. This is pointless."

Though she had no idea what the problem was between them, Paris felt compassion for both men. The
older man was angry and upset and Mac looked as if his
insides were being twisted in a vise.

Looking carefully from one man to the other, she
asked herself why she'd even interfered, but she floun-
dered ahead. "It's lunchtime. They're hungry and will
be ready for a nap soon."

"All right," Mac finally answered. "Let's go." He
started to turn away, but the shorter man reached out and
grabbed Mac's arm.

"I'm not finished talking to you, Weston," he said.

Mac went very still as he looked into the man's eyes,
then down at the hand that gripped his forearm. Without
lifting his voice, he said, "Yes, Burt, you are," in a tone
rich with purpose. "You had a heart attack two years
ago. You don't need to be upsetting yourself like this."

"Then I'd better not see you around anymore," Burt
answered. "Seeing you out and free like you don't have
a care in the world, while my boy is—"

"While your boy is paying for what he did," Mac

were growing up, I was the one [...]
pranks we got into. It was my idea [...]
the concrete business because I war[...]
depend on. I knew he'd gambled [...]
he was over it. I wanted to help [...]
a couple of other businesses t[...]
his head, straightened, and [...]
him, all right, straight int[...]

Mystified, Paris stare[...]
yourself for that? Be[...]
shoddy work on the [...]
it collapsed, but y[...]

"I should hav[...]
having problem[...]
had never af[...]
it came time[...]
look the other w[...]
for Fred, too, and th[...]
going on. And the money [...]
amount, obviously well wort[...]

"That's horrible." Paris couldn[...]
age of the collapsing school out of [...]
happened to them?"

"Fred lost his contractor's license, Steve los[...]
and they both went to jail for a while. They'll be [...]
soon."

"And you, Mac? What happened to you?" she asked
softly, though she already knew the answer.

"I didn't go to jail, but I was financially liable," Mac
answered honestly. "I lost my reputation, my business,
everything but this house, which I'm going to hang
onto—to irritate my former friends in Cliffside if for no
other reason." Kneeling, he returned to his weed-
pulling.

---

finished for him, still in that quiet voi[...]
accepted that, Burt, and quit grieving [...]
over it."

Burt's bottom lip quivered and h[...]
with tears. "Get out of here," he [...]
Mac said, "Burt, you don't own [...]
town."

Burt's jaw shook as if he was trying to form mo[...]
words. Shakily, he turned away, leading his dog. Paris managed
to clear her throat and find her voice. "What *did* he tell
you?"

As he walked away and said, "Just remember what I told you."

"Basically, that this town's not big enough for the
both of us," Mac growled, then he focused his gaze on
her. "And I don't need you to intercede in an argument."

Her lips pinched together sardonically. "Oh, yes it
would be so much better to let Elly and Simon see you
get into a fight."

"There wasn't going to be a fight. He's an old man.
Father of one of my former best friends." Whirling
around, he stalked toward the sandbox. "Come on.
We're going home."

The children were reluctant to leave the playground,
but when Elly saw the fierce expression on her uncle's
face, her arguments died away and she tugged Simon
along meekly.

No doubt they thought he was angry with them, Paris
thought, letting her annoyance with him show in the way
she gathered up the diaper bag and toys and marched to
the truck. He didn't seem to care. His thoughts were
turned inward, and he barely seemed to take note of her
and the children.

...tched as his big, powerful hands grabbed the ...ds and ripped them from their hiding places between the rocks. Sick dismay filled her. She'd known about his situation, but hearing it from him seemed so much harsher because he tried to fight down the emotions that must have plagued him ever since he'd learned of his friends' betrayal.

"Why does Burt, and the rest of the Dexter family, and all of Cliffside seem to blame you?"

Mac answered with a humorless laugh. "Like I said, I was the leader. I was the one who was supposed to keep them out of trouble, and somehow it's not enough that I lost almost everything."

She gaped at him. "You can't win, can you? People are against you on both sides."

"Welcome to my hometown," he said sardonically. "I'm not going to let this rule my life," he added suddenly, fiercely. "I won't let Elly and Simon be around that bitterness." He paused, then gave a deep sigh, and said, "I didn't tell you earlier, but I received a phone call from Sheila this morning while you were in the shower."

"Oh?"

Mac shook his head and laughed mirthlessly. "She didn't have much to say except to prattle on and on about how much she loved working with Roger, that's her new boyfriend, the photographer. She hardly said a thing about her kids."

"Oh, I'm sorry, Mac. She doesn't know what she's missing, and—"

"I don't think she cares." Mac's eyes went dark as he looked at her. "The point is that I'll have the kids for a while and even when she comes back, I'm going to stay in their lives. I'm determined to rebuild my busi-

---

...ulously.

"That was Burt Dexter," Paris repeated, frowning. Wh... heard that name before? "Oh, is he related to Dexter? I met her at Becky's store."

"Dexter," he responded, and she recalled the day he'd found her there with Marva and the Lyte brothers trying to outdo each other in telling her of his "crimes."

"I know,"

Mac grabbed another fistful of grass and yanked it out. "Her husband, Pete was Burt's brother. Their son Fred and Burt's son Steve, were my best friends. Growing up we were always together, the three amigos, the three stooges. When we grew up, we worked together, the three signed buildings and contracted them, read us the riot act crete work, Steve inspected them, Fred did the con- and fined us if everything wasn't exactly to code," Paris said.

"That sounds like a good arrangement, and he dragged

"It was until Fred started gambling and he dragged Steve in with him. Their families blame me."

"Why? You had nothing to do with it."

"Because I'd always been the ringleader. When we

ness and my reputation so that Elly and Simon won't have to grow up defending me, but I'll be damned before I'll let someone like Burt, or anyone else in this town try to hurt them."

"It's horrible," Paris said softly.

"You have no idea," Mac answered.

Paris felt heartsick at the way he said it and couldn't help drawing parallels between his situation and Keith's. Her husband had also been betrayed by his friends. She understood how Mac felt, but he would never know that if she didn't tell him.

"It's rotten when your friends turn on you," she continued quietly. "That's what happened to my husband."

Mac looked around. He gave her a quick, assessing glance as if asking what had prompted this revelation. She answered with a small shrug that admitted her negligence in telling him about herself.

"What happened?" he asked. Turning, he sat down on one of the large rocks and gestured with his open palm in an invitation for her to join him.

Paris had grabbed a jacket on her way out the door behind Mac. She gathered it around her now and sat down. She propped her chin on her hand and stared out at the ocean for a few minutes.

"Keith and I got married right out of high school," she said, speaking in a slow, reflective voice. "That's what way too many kids do in a small town like Hadley. Somehow we tend to think we're not part of a larger world and that we don't have other options." She shook her head. "Silly kids in love. Keith and I were both only children, accustomed to getting whatever we wanted, spoiled and self-centered. Keith had already inherited a large sum of money from his grandparents, and then got even more when his parents retired and left the family citrus-growing business to him. My parents had a smaller farm where I grew up. It was comfortable, but certainly not luxurious. Keith and I were all of twenty-two years old and we were rolling in money." She turned her hands palm-upward. "The only thing worse than a couple of young fools is a couple of young fools with more money than is good for them."

"Spending your own money isn't a crime, Paris," Mac said when she'd been silent for several seconds.

"No, but wastefulness is a crime against a person's soul." She looked up, her green eyes full of regret. "Keith and I began to think that the money would always be there, that it somehow regenerated itself without any care or attention from us. Keith neglected his business and I encouraged him to do so."

Mac was staring at her as if he couldn't picture it. She couldn't blame him. Paris, herself, had a hard time remembering that wasteful, selfish girl.

"So the money ran out?" Mac prompted.

"With the help of our 'friends'," she answered, giving the word an unsavory twist. "It wasn't long before everyone Keith knew had a get-rich-quick scheme that they were sure would turn into a bonanza with a little bit, or a lot, of his money. When I saw this happening, I finally came to my senses, but I couldn't make Keith see that he was throwing away our future. His father even came back from his retirement in San Diego and tried to talk to Keith, but he wouldn't listen. He'd been giving away money for years and it was just too hard to stop. He'd never been a popular boy in high school because he was very quiet and shy, and he knew no world outside of Hadley, didn't really want to. After all, he was a big fish in a small pond, an important young man in town. In truth, he didn't have the head for business his father had, but he could buy his friends, and that's just what he did.''

Paris fell silent as the pain washed over her. Her distress and sorrow still lay like a stone in her heart, weighing her down because she felt there should have been more she could have done to stop him.

She turned her hands over and stared at her empty palms as if picturing all the happiness that had slipped through her fingers. ''Eventually he'd been cheated out of everything. He even had to sell the family home, the business, and the citrus-growing and packing plant that had built the town of Hadley at the turn of the century. There was nothing left except lots of bad investments and debts. None, absolutely none of the get-rich-quick schemes paid off.''

''They never do,'' Mac pointed out. ''Just ask Fred and Steve.''

She turned her face to him, her eyes bruised with sorrowful memories. ''I know. In fact, I knew that then, but Keith couldn't be dissuaded from investing in them. He felt like such a fool, betrayed by the ones he'd thought were his friends—'' She broke off as she looked up at Mac in dismay.

Like you. The unspoken words hung between them. A flicker of Mac's eyes told her he knew what she was thinking.

Paris cleared her throat self-consciously and went on. ''Keith couldn't salvage anything and when he realized that, he just gave up. Strange, but I felt like he was almost glad when he got sick with flu that settled in his chest. It turned into pneumonia and it killed him.'' She looked up at Mac, her green eyes sad. ''The type of pneumonia he had doesn't kill people unless they want it to.''

Mac contemplated her agonized expression and regretted the comments he'd made about her country club lifestyle on the day they'd met. That life certainly hadn't brought her the joy and fulfillment she'd obviously expected—exactly as his success, his beautiful fiancée, and his oceanside home hadn't brought him the joy and fulfillment he'd expected. He watched her shoulders droop as if buckling under the burden of sorrow and guilt she felt for her late husband.

"I'm sorry, Paris," he said awkwardly. "It must have been hell for you. Is that why you left your hometown?"

She nodded, her bright hair sifting down over her face. "There was nothing left for me there; no family, few friends." She looked up swiftly as if she was going to say something further, then subsided and glanced away almost as if she was hiding guilt. "I didn't want contact with them. That's why I used a high school friend, Carolyn, as a reference. She'd never been part of what had happened to Keith, had never come to him asking for money so I knew she wouldn't have a reason to give me a bad reference. You see, I made a lot of people in Hadley mad once I started trying to convince my husband not to squander his money. Our money."

It still hurt that people had turned on her. She knew exactly how Mac felt, but she'd begun coming to terms with what she had allowed to happen to her.

What on earth could she have to feel guilty about? *She* was the one who had been hurt, Mac thought furiously.

"It took me a while to get everything cleared up." She glanced up and flashed him a wobbly smile. "It's ironic that you've got this big, empty house sitting here on the coast and I've got a storage facility full of furniture in Hadley. There were things of my family's that

I couldn't part with so I stored them. Besides, I had all that stuff I'd bought. It's of excellent quality. I should have sold it, but I didn't. Apathy, I guess, but in a way all that stuff ties me to the past.''

"You'll probably want them someday."

"I suppose I might," she said slowly, as if she hadn't really considered it. That was another irony, she thought. He did nothing but think about the future and how he could affect it, and she seemed hardly to consider hers.

After a moment, Paris spoke again. "Anyway, when I was finished with that, I packed everything I thought I would need in my car and started north. That was a year ago. Since then, I've worked all kinds of jobs, ones I didn't think I could do."

"Like being a nanny?"

She shrugged and gave a small laugh. "Yes, but I've turned out to be pretty good at that. Wouldn't the people of Hadley be surprised?"

He was stunned to realize that his hand was reaching out to her in an offer of comfort. He drew it back and stared at her bowed head in perplexity. He was the last person who ought to be offering comfort. There was none in him to give. He knew that, and yet he felt as if something was changing inside him, softening and giving way like an earthen dam pummeled by too much rain. He didn't want to feel what he was experiencing. How could he stay mad at the world, stay focused on his goal of paying off his debts and rebuilding his business and reputation if he let himself feel pity?

And yet, he wanted her. He'd been jealous when she'd gone out with Grey. He'd wanted to make love to her, to fold her around him in comfort, to give her comfort, but how could he? Hadn't that ability died when he'd given his all to his ambition, focused so strongly on his goal that every other consideration of life was blotted out?

Mac rubbed the back of his hand across his mouth, aware for the first time that maybe his goal was an empty one. No, he thought suddenly, fiercely. It couldn't be that he'd spent so much time thinking about this, planning it for nothing.

Unwilling to think about that further, he gave her an uncomfortable look as he murmured, "Will you ever go back there?"

"No," she answered firmly. "There's nothing for me there. I wouldn't be welcome, and it would hurt too much." She paused, and then looked up to meet his gaze. "What about you, Mac? Will you ever forgive the people in Cliffside?"

He frowned at her. "Forgive them?" He'd never thought in those terms. "What for?"

"They were your friends, people you'd known all your life, but they believed the worst of you."

Mac gave a bark of mirthless laughter. "You think they'd want my forgiveness? Get real. Nobody in town cares."

"Not for them, Mac," Paris said gently. "For you. For your sake."

"I don't need that," he said, making a cutting gesture with the side of his hand. "I need to be left alone."

She gave him an exasperated look. "It's true that time heals all wounds, or at least grows a scab over them, but there should be a way to speed up the process. Until you see that you need to forgive these people and get past your anger, that healing is never going to take place."

Mac stood facing her with his hands resting lightly at his waist and his head thrust forward. His jaw was set, his brows drawn together in a frown, and his eyes stormy as they looked her over. "You sound like a preacher," he said.

Heat rushed into Paris's face, turning it bright red. Angry and embarrassed that he wouldn't even listen to her, she said, "I'm only telling you what I've learned in the past couple of years. Bitterness doesn't hurt anyone except the one who's bitter."

"Oh, knock it off. Now you sound like a psychologist."

"Better than wallowing in self-pity," she snapped.

"Self-pity?" He looked at her as if he couldn't believe his ears. He pointed his finger at her. "I guarantee you that's the last thing I'm feeling."

"Oh, really? What would you call it, then?" She ticked off a list on her fingers. "You hid out from the town until your niece and nephew came to stay, and even then, you didn't want them to go near the people in Cliffside."

"I told you why."

Paris ignored him. "You don't let people get close to you, it seems to me, unless they prove themselves worthy."

"That's a load of bull," Mac said, his voice low with fury. "I hired you, didn't I, in spite of that pitiful excuse for a work record?"

Fury made her voice tremble. "Well, I guess the next question is whether or not I've proven myself worthy, isn't it, Mac?"

He leaned close to her, his eyes narrow, his voice coarse. "I guess you have. I wanted to sleep with you, didn't I?"

Hurt punched her in the stomach, draining all the color from her face. Appalled, she took a step away from him. Slowly, she shook her head from side to side as if she couldn't quite take in what he'd said.

A sick look came over his face, too, and he lifted his hand as if to draw her back to him.

Paris stumbled away, turned and fled into the house.

CHAPTER TEN

"PARIS." Horrified at what he'd said, Mac called after her, but she slammed the door as he rounded the corner of the house. His hand shot out to shove the door open. Whose house was this, anyway? She had no right to slam a door in his face.

But then he let his hand fall away. Who was he kidding? He'd been vile to her. He deserved a lot worse than a slammed door. Sick at heart, disgusted with himself, he returned to his weed-pulling, ripping the stubborn grass out furiously and wishing he could rip out the words he'd said.

God, what was the matter with him? He'd never before hurt anyone intentionally, no matter what the citizens of Cliffside might think, and...

When that thought flashed through his mind, Mac sprang upright as if someone had kicked him. Was she right? Had he sunk into self-pity so far that every one of his thoughts circled back to Cliffside, to the people there and how they'd wronged him?

Bitterness doesn't hurt anyone except the one who's bitter.

He wasn't bitter. Bitterness was a dead end, a road that led nowhere, unproductive and unfulfilling.

Like self-pity.

"Oh, hell," he blasted the words out as he bent and wrestled more devil grass out of its hiding place. Too bad he couldn't wrestle out the memory of Paris's words as easily.

"Oooh," Paris lamented as she stomped into the kitchen. She ought to slam the door again, just for good measure, to let him know how furious she was with him. She stormed around the kitchen instead, from the refrigerator to the window to the stove where she picked up the stainless steel teakettle and considered taking it outside and chucking it at his head. Nah, if she did that, she'd have to get close to him again. Her aim wasn't that great from a distance. She whacked the teakettle back to the stovetop, splashing water up and out of the spout.

She took another turn around the room and ended up at the window. Realizing she could see him working out there, pulling up unwelcome plants and tossing them aside as easily as he seemed to want to toss her and her feelings aside.

It infuriated her that he was working away as if what he'd said was nothing important, not devastating to her, or even hurtful. Incoherent with rage, she marched into the living room and glared out the plate glass windows at the ocean far below.

"I wanted to sleep with you, didn't I?"

How could he have said such an odious thing, as if the love she felt for him was cheap? More than cheap, worthless. True, he didn't know she loved him, but he knew what kind of woman she was—that she was warm and loving, conscientious and thoughtful, that she was still working to overcome a situation very similar to his. He knew her, didn't he?

Frustrated, she lifted her hands to her head and ran her fingers through her hair. Didn't he know her? Maybe not. It was obvious that he didn't know she'd kissed him because she cared about him.

What did he think all that had been about? she wondered as she stared unseeing out at the water that rippled and flashed in the sunshine. Did he think she was a lonely, sex-starved widow?

No. Paris reached up and rubbed the heels of her hands against her eyes. It was exactly as she had told him. For him, people had to prove themselves worthy, over and over and over again before he could accept them or accept love or affection from them. Perhaps he hadn't always been that way. After all, he'd cared for his parents, taken on the raising of his sister, taken in her children. Was that love, though, or just taking care of his responsibilities?

Heartsick, she concluded that he wouldn't want her love. She was wasting her time here.

She didn't have to stay, Paris thought, wheeling away from the awesome view. She could leave. In the past year, she'd left a lot of places; her hometown, her home, sad memories, even her happy ones. Leaving pigheaded, thoughtless Mac Weston would be a snap.

Determined to pack and flee right away, Paris rushed down the hall to her room. As she did so, her gaze automatically swung to the children's room as it always did when she passed. She caught a glimpse of Elly, half-on and half-off of her bed.

Halted in her headlong flight, Paris caught herself against the edge of the doorjamb and looked at the little girl. Elly's chubby arms were flung wide, one trailing off the bed, her dimpled leg flung across so that the next movement would send her tumbling onto the floor.

A rush of compassion surged through Paris, taking the edge off her fury with Mac. Gently, she tiptoed into the room and turned Elly onto her stomach away from the edge of the bed, then tucked a pillow up against her back so she wouldn't roll off again. The youngster's arm flopped onto her stuffed rabbit and she snuggled it close.

Turning, Paris peeked into the crib where Simon lay curled with his cheek on one of his books, his fiery hair forming damp curls around his forehead.

Funny little squirt, she thought affectionately. Most kids cuddled stuffed toys like Elly's rabbit, but this one adored books.

Paris took a deep breath to help clear her mind. She knew she couldn't leave them, especially not this abruptly. She loved them. Sure, Mac could find someone else to take care of them. Becky's mother, June, might even be willing to do it, but they didn't need another change like that. They'd had enough upheavals in the past few weeks.

Her anger with him began to ease and she was able to think more clearly. The sick disappointment she felt with Mac still haunted her, but she could deal with that. She'd done it before.

Paris knew she couldn't run away again, not as long as she was needed here. She had to stay. But it was going to be on her own terms. Mac might be the boss, but he wasn't going to have things strictly his way anymore.

Weighed down by an iciness she had hoped never to feel again, Paris left the children's room and went to her own. Pulling out the journal she hadn't written in for several days, she curled up on her bed and wrote down all her thoughts about Mac. As she wrote, she formed a plan.

"I need to talk to you."

Mac turned around. He'd been expecting this all evening. Paris had cooked and served dinner in an atmosphere cold enough to freeze boiling oil. He might have voiced that thought aloud, but he didn't want to give her any ideas regarding boiling oil.

She had showered and dressed in snug jeans and a coral sweater that cast a warm glow over her skin. Her hair was pulled back in a ponytail that made her look like the teenager that the hapless Keith Barbour had fallen in love with. She was so beautiful she made him ache but she barely spared a glance in his direction.

For the past hour, she had only brightened when the children were around, but now that they were playing quietly in the living room, she seemed to feel free to let him have it.

Mac turned around and squared his shoulders. Let her do her worst. He deserved it. "Yes, Paris, what is it?"

She folded her hands at her waist in a way that reminded him of his third grade teacher. Her face was as cool and composed as a plaster saint. "As soon as you have hired a competent nanny, I'm going to make plans to leave—"

"Paris, I—"

She held up her hand. "Please let me finish. I expect a letter of recommendation from you. I think I've done a good job here and I've provided a stable environment for the children. I can do the same thing in another nannying job, but it will look better if I have a recommendation from you."

"Of...of course," he stammered. "But you don't have to leave." The idea filled him with dread bordering on panic. Why had he said such a vicious thing to her? She wouldn't even let him apologize. Every time he tried, she cut him off.

She lifted an eyebrow at him. "After you've hired another nanny, why would I stay?"

Good question. Darned good question. She wouldn't stay for his sake. He'd guaranteed that.

He couldn't let her go. He knew that as clearly as he knew he'd hurt her.

He wasn't going to let it end this way, he decided with sudden determination. "I might still need a housekeeper," he said, grasping at straws.

"I'm sure you'll have no trouble finding someone else."

This was like talking to a block of granite. Stepping forward, he said, "Paris, I'm sorry for what I said. I was acting like a jerk."

"Yes," she agreed quietly. "You were." She looked up and met his gaze. The hurt he saw there kicked him right in the gut. "You don't have to agree with what I said, Mac, you don't even have to listen to me, but you haven't been listening to anyone or anything except your anger for a long time. That's your problem, not mine, but you don't have to take it out on me."

"Paris, I didn't mean..." But he *had* meant it and they both knew it. He didn't know what else to say because anything he came up with she lobbed right back at him with a massive rock of truth attached. He decided to shut his mouth before he got any more bruises.

When he didn't go on, Paris turned and left the room to invite Elly and Simon for a walk. She found their jackets and the three of them went out, leaving him behind. Watching them go, Mac wondered how he'd managed to mess things up so badly. Somehow the loss he was feeling was worse than what he'd been through when his two best friends had betrayed him. At least then he hadn't been at fault. And his heart hadn't been involved.

* * *

By the time Mac left for work on Monday morning, Paris felt as if the tension inside her was wound tightly enough to choke her. She wasn't sure she could do this anymore, she thought as she listened to his truck rumble up the driveway to the road.

She'd given such a cool and brave talk about staying until he hired another nanny, but when would that be? He could stretch it out for years if he wanted and she loved the children so much she might stick around that long for fear they wouldn't be cared for by someone who truly loved them.

Paris knew she couldn't live that long in the same house with a man she loved, but who didn't love her. The tension would drive her mad. She saw no way out of it, though.

"Come on, Pris," Elly called out, padding down the hallway in her pajamas. Her hair was a tangled mass around her head and her stuffed rabbit bumped her heels as she walked. "We gotta get ready so we can go see Becky."

Paris scooped the little girl into her arms and laid her cheek on her fragrant hair. "You're right. And we can go to the park, too."

The only good thing about this weekend was that Mac had dropped his objections to her taking the children into Cliffside. Maybe he felt that every bad situation that could happen had already done so and that he should stop trying to avoid it. It meant she could find some playmates for Elly and Simon. She intended to start by talking to Becky about it as she had intended to so many days ago.

By midmorning, she and the children were walking up the steps of Becky's store. As usual, Floyd and Benny were outside, only this time, they were sitting on a couple of chairs that they had leaned up against the front of the building. Paris cast them a sidelong glance, wishing they weren't always hanging around.

Grumpily, she wondered if there was a local job education program that could use them on a poster. The caption could say, "Get the training and education you need or you could turn out like this."

Elly scooted close to Paris when she saw them. Paris reached down to get a firm grip on her hand, hitched Simon higher on her hip, and marched past them. As she passed through the door, she heard two loud thumps and knew the men were going to follow her inside. With a mental sigh, she tried to think how to deal with the situation. After the nerve-wracking weekend she'd spent, she wasn't sure she could be polite to them.

The tinkle of the old-fashioned bell brought Becky to the front of the store and she smiled broadly when she saw the children. "Hey kidlets," she said. "Come give Auntie Becky a hug."

Elly didn't wait for a second invitation. She streaked down the aisle and wrapped herself around Becky's legs.

Laughing, Becky bent to pick her up. "What have you two been up to?"

Elly rolled her eyes toward the ceiling and frowned. "Oh, we went up to the hill on a walk and now we came up to the store."

Becky and Paris laughed together at her literal answer and Elly beamed back at them. They were interrupted when the bell sounded again and the Lyte brothers thudded into the store.

Becky's lips pinched together as she turned toward the counter to find a treat for the children. "Benny and Floyd, if you're going to buy something, you're welcome. If not, you can go right back out the door you came in.''

Becky's bluntness didn't stop them. The two men trudged up to Paris. ''Hello, Ms. Barbour,'' Floyd said, his small eyes giving her an interested look. ''Where's Mac today?''

''Where most people are on a Monday morning,'' she answered pointedly. ''At work.'' She might be hurt and disappointed with Mac, but she still loved him and she wouldn't let these two say anything bad about him.

''Well, he's lucky to have the freedom to be at work and not in jail,'' Floyd smirked.

Paris lifted her eyebrows at him. This was sudden. After weeks of innuendoes, Benny was bluntly stating what was on his mind. She wondered if he'd been talking to Burt Dexter. ''Why on earth should he be in jail for something someone else did?''

''There's people in this town that think he knew all about what Fred and Steve were doing. After all, the three of them had done everything together since they were kids.''

His brother nodded at this statement.

Paris started to answer but was interrupted by yet another ring of the bell. She glanced up to see Burt Dexter, followed by his sister-in-law, Marva, coming into the room. Oh, great, she thought with an inward sigh. The entire Hate Mac Weston committee had arrived.

''Down,'' Simon grunted, starting to wiggle. Usually content to be carried, he'd spotted the candy Becky was handing out to his sister and he wanted his share. Paris set him on the floor and watched him totter away.

She exchanged looks with Becky, whose fierce expression said she was ready to leap over the counter and throw them all out bodily. With a tiny shake of her head, Paris discouraged that and turned back to the two men.

"It doesn't necessarily follow that he knew anything about what his two best friends were doing," Paris pointed out, keeping her voice steady and reasonable in spite of the anger that was beginning to flare inside her.

"Well, I—" Floyd began, but she cut him off.

"Has it occurred to you, or anyone else in this town, that you all seem to be stuck in a time warp? You can't move past something that happened two *years* ago. What does that say about you, Floyd?" Turning her head, she looked at the Dexter family and was washed with pity. They'd been humiliated and wanted someone to blame.

"It seems to me that Mac is the only one who *has* moved past this," she went on.

Outside, Mac paused with his hand on the screen door, ready to push it open. He couldn't believe his ears. Paris was defending him. He'd been on his way into Alban to pick up more roof tiles when he'd spotted Paris's car in front of Becky's store. He'd turned in, for once with no thought of dragging his family away from town, but instead because he'd wanted to see them. He'd spent hours pounding nails that morning and had reached the conclusion that he'd been enough of a fool. He wanted to talk to Paris. It sounded, though, like she was doing all the talking.

He paused to listen, ready to rush in at the first sign of conflict.

"You don't know what you're talking about," Burt Dexter said.

"Oh? Who is it that sold almost everything to fulfill what he saw as his responsibility?"

"It *was* his responsibility," Floyd said.

"Because he felt he owed it to the community, but he

wasn't paying for his own crime. He was paying for someone else's.'' She looked at the Dexter family, who couldn't meet her eyes. "He was paying for the crimes of his best friends.''

No one answered. The room was so quiet Paris could hear Simon noisily sucking on the candy Becky had given him.

Strangely, as she talked, she felt something turn loose inside her. She had accused Mac of bitterness, but she'd harbored it, too. Hers wasn't only against the friends who had cheated her husband, but against Keith, too, and against the girl she used to be, the witless one who hadn't stopped her husband from squandering their future. She had to forgive all those people, stop letting her bitterness drag her down, and move on.

She lifted her eyes in an appeal to the people facing her. "Isn't it time to let this die and get on with life? This animosity isn't helping anyone.'' She turned to Floyd who was still glaring at her defiantly. "What did you and your brother do to help the town recover from the collapse of the school?''

He drew back, offended. "Hey, we had nothing to do with that.''

"And you didn't do anything to solve it, either,'' Burt Dexter broke in. "None of us did.''

"We were humiliated,'' Marva added. Her face pinkened and she looked away.

"And it was easier to blame Mac than our sons,'' Burt finished up.

"It's not too late to change things.'' Mac spoke from outside, then opened the door and walked in. When his eyes met Paris's across the room, he shrugged and lifted his hands. "All this anger and bitterness isn't doing anyone any good. Why don't we just drop it? I'm getting damned tired of avoiding my own hometown.''

Burt gave Mac a shamefaced look, turned and walked to him with his hand outstretched. ''It's been my fault, Mac. I've kept the bitterness alive because I couldn't admit that Fred and Steve had done wrong. Even after the trial I denied it. What you said in the park the other day was right, though. I can't get upset like that anymore. If I don't let go of this, it's going to kill me.''

Mac reached out and shook the older man's hand. ''Yeah,'' he said, one corner of his mouth tilting up. ''Someone pointed out to me that bitterness only hurts the person who's bitter.''

Burt nodded then turned to leave, holding the door for Marva as he went. She patted Mac's arm, gave Paris a small smile, and left the store.

Floyd and Benny were right behind them, but Benny stopped to say, ''When you get back in the designing and building business, Mac, give us a call. We wouldn't mind working for you.'' Floyd gave his brother a disgusted look, but he didn't contradict him.

''Sure, Ben,'' Mac said, but his expression told Paris that he felt as if he'd been damned with faint praise. ''If you two can work me into your schedule, I'll be glad to have your help.''

The irony of that statement went unnoticed by the two men as they clumped out the door.

''Well, I'll be darned,'' Becky said, bringing the children out from behind the counter. ''I never thought I'd see that.'' She breathed a huge sigh of relief. ''I think things are going to be a lot better around this town from now on.''

Mac started to answer her, but Elly rushed up to him,

clamoring for his attention with Simon right behind, holding his sticky face up for a kiss from his uncle.

Tears welled in Paris's eyes. Everything she'd wanted for Mac had happened within a space of a few minutes. She wanted to tell him how proud she felt, how relieved that he had begun to make peace with his old friends.

"I want lunch," Elly announced, looking from one adult to another, then she gave a sly look. "Becky has sandwiches over there, and soda pop."

"Sod pop," Simon agreed, nodding.

Mac laughed. "Why don't we go home and have lunch?" He reached out and slipped his arm around Paris's waist. "I need to talk to Paris in private."

"What's in private mean?" Elly asked.

"That means without nosy little girls around," he said, pinching her nose lightly.

Elly giggled as he turned them all toward the door. Becky waved them out and secretly gave an "okay" sign to Paris, who smiled back.

Hurriedly, she secured the children in the car and started home. Mac was right behind them all the way. Whenever Paris glanced into her rearview mirror, she saw him looking at her. That slow, sexy smile of his made her feel lightheaded and breathless—not a condition for safe driving. Paris kept her eyes on the road.

When they reached Mac's house, they hurried inside and Paris began quickly putting sandwiches together. She and Mac moved around the room, getting the meal ready and all the while tension seemed to hum in the air between them.

She wanted to tell him how proud she was of the way he'd handled things in town, that she was glad he and people like the Dexters and the Lytes had begun coming to terms with what had happened to them all.

Mac gave her sidelong glances, and even a wink followed by a grin when he caught her staring at him. To her embarrassment, she blushed and Elly said, "Pris, why is your face all red like that?"

"No reason, Elly," Paris answered, scooping her up and into her chair. Behind her, Mac chuckled.

As she was fixing the children's plates, the phone rang. Mac grabbed it up with one hand as he poured glasses of milk with the other.

"Yeah, Mac Weston here," he said, then went very still. Paris turned to look at him. His gaze met hers, then swung to the children. Somehow Paris knew it was Sheila.

"I need to switch phones," he said to the caller. He handed the receiver to Paris. "Hang this up when I pick it up in the bedroom."

She nodded and watched him stride from the room. Though she was wildly curious to know why Sheila was calling, Paris went through the motions of the meal with the children, making sure they ate at least part of their lunch and drank all their milk. Mac didn't come back by the time they'd finished, so she took Elly and Simon to their room for naptime.

As she passed Mac's room, she heard him in tense conversation, his voice rising and falling in short staccato bursts. By now, she was familiar with all the tones of his voice and this was the angriest she had ever heard him.

Barely able to concentrate, Paris read two books to the children, then insisted they rest. She slipped from the room and down the hall to Mac's where she heard silence.

Opening the door, she found him sitting on the side

of the bed, his head down and shoulders slumped, his hands dangling loosely between his knees.

"Mac?" she asked, coming inside and closing the door behind her. "What's wrong?"

He didn't answer for a long moment, and then he looked up, his face devastated.

Alarmed, Paris hurried to sit beside him. "Mac?"

"It was Sheila. She's giving up." He shook his head slowly then stared into Paris's eyes.

She reached to cover his hands with hers. "Giving up? Giving up what, Mac?"

"Her children. Elly and Simon. She says she's not fit to be their mother. She's got too many other things she wants to do. Her new boyfriend has received some kind of grant to photograph a year in the life of some elephant herd and she's going to be his assistant. After that, who knows? But she doesn't want to be a mommy anymore." Mac blinked and focused. "She's not coming back, Paris. She's giving me legal custody of the kids. I'll probably have them until they're grown. I'm not going to be an uncle now. I'm going to be a father."

Paris could barely take in what he was saying. Her green eyes wide with distress, she said, "You can't be serious."

"Serious as judgment day."

"She's going to give them up like they were..."

"Mongrel puppies," Mac said bitterly. The sick expression in his eyes told Paris that his disappointment in his sister was profound.

Paris's hands tightened on his. "At least they'll be with you, though, Mac. You...you are going to keep them, aren't you?"

"Of course." He looked surprised that she'd even question that.

Relief flooded her and she smiled. "It'll be okay, then. They love you and you love them. It'll work out fine."

"No. No, it won't."

He sounded so positive, she was shocked. "Why ever not?"

His dark eyes snapped as he answered. "Because you won't be here."

At a loss, she said, "I...I said I'd stay for a while, and..." Her voice trailed off. The idea of leaving the children made her sick. The thought of leaving Mac was one she'd tried to reconcile all weekend, but she couldn't live with it, either. She swallowed hard. "I'll stay for a while."

"No." He turned suddenly and his hands turned up, gripping hers. "I don't want you to stay for a while. I want you to stay forever."

"What?" Heat rushed through her. "Mac, I don't think I can..."

"Marry me," he said bluntly.

CHAPTER ELEVEN

"MARRY you?" Paris couldn't have been more shocked if he'd whipped out a hammer and rapped her on the head with it.

"Don't you see? It's the perfect solution." Mac dropped her hands, stood, and began pacing the room, from the door to the window to the dresser and back again. "You love Elly and Simon, don't you?"

"Of...of course, but..."

"You've established a routine for them. It would be easier for them to learn their mother's not coming back if they know you're staying, right?" He stopped his pacing, turned and speared her with a challenging look.

Hardly able to get her breath, she put her hand to her head to stop it spinning. "Yes, but there's more to it than that."

"What?" he asked, throwing his hands wide. "You like it here, don't you? You have no place else to go."

That didn't sound very flattering. She began losing some of her shock. Since she didn't like the disadvantage of sitting while he paced, she stood and faced him while he prowled the room. "I'm hardly an orphan, Mac. I could always have gone to Keith's parents in San Diego. In fact, they wanted me to, and..."

"But do you want to?"

"No, but I don't know that I want to marry you, either. What kind of marriage would that be? Marrying for the sake of two children."

"They need us both."

She thrust her chin out. "There are certain things *I* need, Mac. Remember, I've been married before, so I know what I need in a marriage."

"What?" he asked, appearing truly puzzled, then his eyes cleared. "You mean security, don't you? You're worried about the debt I'm paying off. Don't worry about that. It's almost paid. Things might be a little tight for a few more months, but they'll pick up by next spring. A firm of architects in Alban has asked me to join them. I can do that." He shrugged. "I was stubbornly hanging onto the idea that I needed to be independent, to be my own boss, but they want to make me a partner. I'll be my own boss, but I'll have partners, and I'll never be in this financial situation again. I'll take care of you."

"That's not it, Mac," she said desperately.

He didn't hear the despair in her voice. "You don't have to worry about how we'll provide for Elly and Simon because Sheila's got a trust fund from our father that she's going to turn over to me. She wants to take care of them, but not in a hands-on kind of way."

Paris held up her own hands in a futile attempt to stem the tide of his words. "That's not it, Mac," she repeated.

"It's what I said the other day about sleeping with you because you'd proven yourself. I'm sorry about that, Paris. It was vile...."

"No, Mac."

He frowned. "Then what is it? I've tried to answer any fears you might have."

"What about love?"

Now she was the one who had shocked him. He stared ⁀ her for a full twenty seconds before he echoed, ⁀e?" in a strangled voice.

⁀ou know that emotion people claim to feel for

each other when they decide to marry?'' *The emotion I feel for you,* she thought, but bit the words back.

Mac lifted his hand and rubbed the back of it over his mouth as if he was trying to eradicate the word that was hanging in the air between them. He took a breath. ''Don't you think it's a little overrated, Paris?''

''Overrated?''

''How many people in this country get married in a hormone rush and regret it later? You said yourself that's what you and your husband had done.''

''Oh, Mac, that's hardly the same thing. We were teenagers, for goodness' sake.''

''Maybe, but if you'd stopped to reason things out, list good reasons for marriage like I've just listed for you, would you still have married him?''

He had her there. ''No,'' Paris admitted slowly. ''Probably not.''

''So it's barely possible that love is overrated, hm?''

She raised an eyebrow at him. ''Don't twist my words up with your reasoning, Mac.'' She was already twisted up with wanting to do as he was asking and reluctance to go through with it. No matter what he said, it wouldn't be much of a marriage without love.

While she stood brooding about it, Mac moved up to stand before her. His arms came out to draw her close. ''And there's this,'' he said, quietly closing his mouth over hers.

Yes, she thought blissfully. There was certainly this. Her hands slipped around his waist, fisting into the fabric of his shirt, feeling the strength of his muscle-roped back. His mouth was warm, exciting, sweet, but still she felt as if she was being cheated. What was this physical attraction if it didn't include love? She wanted more than that. Didn't she?

He pulled away and looked down into her eyes, then lifted his hand and smoothed strands of hair away from her face. "I'm going to call my boss and tell him something's come up and I'll be out for the rest of the day, then I'm going to call my lawyer and see what needs to be done to get this permanent custody arrangement made as fast as possible. While I'm doing that, you think about marrying me."

"Okay," she gasped. As if there was a chance of her thinking about anything else! "The kids are napping," she told him, pulling out of his arms because when he held her, her thinking was much too fuzzy. "While they're asleep, I'm going to go...somewhere..."

"And think," he finished for her, then kissed her forehead as if he wanted to put a seal on her good sense.

"And...and think." She stood back, pressed her palms together, then turned and fled from the room. As she hurried through the house, she checked on the children who were sleeping peacefully, then grabbed her purse and dashed out to her car.

As she started the car and roared up the driveway, she thought about driving all the way to San Francisco to do her thinking. When she whipped onto the highway, she thought that maybe a drive to Alban might be enough. By the time she reached Cliffside, she pulled into the parking lot of Becky's store and was halfway out of the car before she realized what she was doing. It seemed right, though, so she barreled up the steps and into the store, letting the screen door slam behind her.

She stood, looking around in a dazed way at the few customers who were there. They gazed back at her in a frozen tableau while she sought out Becky, who came down an aisle to meet her, then rushed forward when she saw Paris's face.

"What's wrong? Did something happen when you left here? Is Mac all right? The kids?"

Paris nodded. "They're...okay, but..." She gulped, stopped, and burst into tears.

"Oh my gosh." Becky whipped around, grabbed a box of tissues off a shelf and shoved them into Paris's shaking hands. "Sorry, folks," she called out. "There's something I've got to take care of so I've got to close up for a little while."

She hustled everyone out in record time and locked the door behind them. Paris, busy sobbing into a handful of tissues, looked up and said, "I'm sorry...your customers...Benny and Floyd, they aren't..."

Becky put her arm around Paris's shoulders and urged her upstairs and into her apartment. "Don't worry about them. I told them if they didn't get off my porch, I was going to start making them pay rent. That moved them out fast enough. I wish I'd done that months ago, but I felt sorry for them. I was a sap. Now, tell me what's wrong with you." She took Paris into her tiny living room, seated her on the couch, and sat down beside her.

"I was a s...sa...hap, too," Paris wailed. "I fell in love with Mac."

"You did?" Becky asked in a careful tone, though she didn't sound surprised.

"And that's not all. There's...there's something worse." Paris swiped at her eyes.

"Worse?"

"He...a...ask...asked me to mar...marry him."

Becky's eyes widened. "The unforgivable cad."

Paris nodded. "That's what I thought."

"Uh, *why* did you think that?"

"I just told you. Because I luh...love him." Paris

broke into loud sobs and Becky patted her shoulders in comfort.

"That's terrible," Becky sympathized, then murmured, "I guess," in a puzzled tone.

"It *is* terrible," Paris said, gesturing with a handful of damp tissues. "Because he doesn't love me. He says love is overrated. That most people get married in a hormone rush and…and wouldn't get married at all if they stopped to think about it."

"He's probably right."

Paris stared at Becky through watery eyes. "You don't agree with him, do you?"

"Honey, it doesn't matter if I agree with him. *You're* the one who has to agree."

"Well, I don't," Paris said, flopping back against the couch.

"Why not?"

"Because I want love."

"And you think it comes in only one form?"

Paris blinked at her friend. "Huh?"

Becky stood and moved to her small kitchen area where she poured glasses of cola for both of them. "Paris," she said after a few minutes of silence. "Ever since I met you, I was glad you were in Mac's life even if it was only as a temporary housekeeper and nanny." She handed Paris a glass. "Drink up," she said. "You need a jolt of sugar and caffeine."

Dutifully, Paris gulped a mouthful.

"Like I was saying," Becky went on. "I was glad you were in Mac's life because you're one of the most levelheaded, steady people I've ever met. It can't have been easy living with him, taking care of two kids you didn't know, that he didn't want to get to know for fear he'd love them and lose them. But you did it and I admire that in you. He admires it, too, but he probably doesn't know how to say it.''

Paris nodded. ''Go on.''

''The point I'm trying to make is that he trusts you. He hasn't trusted anyone in more than two years. He couldn't afford to, his friends betrayed him, his town turned on him, his fiancée cleaned out his house and dumped him, his sister deposited two kids with him. Right now, trust is all he has to give.''

''Are you saying that's equal to love?''

''In a roundabout way,'' Becky admitted. ''Love builds on trust.''

''Are you saying I should marry him?''

Becky waved a hand at her. ''I wouldn't presume to tell you what to do. You've got to make up your own mind.''

Paris's tears were drying rapidly as Becky's words began to make sense to her. Hope began to glimmer inside her. If he had trust and she had love, maybe that would be enough on which to build a marriage. It was a more mature start than she and Keith had when they'd married.

Becky, sensing the struggle going on in Paris, said, ''Drink your cola, then go on home and tell Mac your decision. Whatever it is, you're not going to hurt him, the children, or yourself.''

Paris nodded, then smiled tremulously, realizing that the two of them had cemented their friendship and it wouldn't be affected by what she chose to do about Mac's proposal. Lifting her glass, she toasted Becky, who grinned and winked at her. ''In case the subject comes up, I've got a dress that would make a heck of a maid of honor's dress.''

Where was she? Mac prowled to the front window and gazed out, then stalked through the house and peered out at the driveway. One way or another, he'd done his share of pacing today.

He shouldn't have let her go, he thought morosely. He should have locked her in her room until she agreed to marry him. Too bad her bedroom door didn't have an outside lock on it.

He'd gone about it all wrong. Sure he wanted to marry her so he could have the best environment for the kids, and she had a right to know that up front, but he should have made it sound more romantic. Women liked romantic things; candlelight, roses, wine, proposals on bended knee. He could have done all that. Well, maybe not the bended knee part. That might have been taking things a little too far. He should have done a better job of it, though.

Elly, awake from her nap, but still sleepy, came up, tucked her hand into his, and leaned against his leg, hugging her rabbit to her chest. "Where's Pris?" she asked. "I want her to come home now."

Mac turned, picked his niece up, and sat on a kitchen chair with her on his lap. "Me too," he said, marveling at the way she laid her bright head against his chest and curled against him as if she had every reason to think nothing would ever happen to her as long as she was with him. Couldn't Paris be that way? Couldn't she trust him to take care of her?

He scoffed at himself. He was being naive. What a grown woman wanted was far different than what a four-year-old wanted. His throat felt tight as he said, "She'll be home soon."

"Good," Elly said, and yawned. "I saw a bird outside

I need to tell her about. She likes it when I tell her things."

"Well, so do I," he said, and kissed the top of her head. "Tell me."

Elly launched into a story about a bluejay she'd seen outside her bedroom window and how it was lost and looking for its family. While she talked, Mac heard echoes of her own fears and knew he was doing the right thing in moving heaven and earth to give her and Simon the home they needed.

He'd talked to his lawyer who was setting the wheels in motion. Mac wanted to push for adoption, but knew he'd have to settle for legal custody first.

He had made an appointment with a child psychologist who he hoped would give him some advice on how to tell the children that they were going to be staying with him. And with Paris, he hoped. And prayed, he thought, with a sense of shock. He wanted her to be his wife as much as he wanted to keep Elly and Simon for his own. It amounted to the first soul-deep prayer he'd said in years.

Elly broke off her story in midsentence. "There she is," she said, leaping down from Mac's lap and dashing to the door when she heard Paris's car crunching gravel in the driveway. She tried to turn the knob, but Mac wouldn't open the door for her until Paris had stopped the car. When he let Elly out, she danced forward and into Paris's welcoming arms. Laughing, Paris scooped her up and kissed her while Elly threw her arms round her neck and exclaimed, "I missed you soooo much, Pris. I thought you weren't coming back."

"Hey, don't be a silly girl," Paris chided lovingly. "I came back. I'll always come back. I wouldn't go off and leave my Elly." She glanced up then and met Mac's eyes. The smile she gave him was so pure and sweet, it made him feel like an undeserving fool.

That's when it hit him, when all the feelings he'd had churning in him for weeks now twisted around and made sense. It was exactly like the moment when a design he'd carried in his head was laid out on the drafting board in perfect alignment.

This was why he'd said love was overrated. Because he didn't know what it really was. He hadn't loved Judith—he'd only told himself he did because she was beautiful and accomplished. He'd never loved anyone before this moment. That's why he'd been jealous of Grey, why he'd wanted to keep Paris with him, to make love to her. Because he was *in* love with her.

His eyes on Paris, he tried to think of something to say to make up for the awkward proposal he'd made earlier. Thinking about it now made him wince. He hadn't said any of the things he should have said.

"I've got to go get Simon up," Elly said. "He was worried about you, too."

Paris set her on the ground, and the little girl scurried inside. Slowly, Paris followed, her eyes on Mac. She stopped in the doorway where he stood and looked up into his eyes. "I've finished thinking, Mac." She took a deep breath. "Yes, I'll marry you."

All the tension drained out of him. Shaking, he reached for her hands as he said the only logical thing and watched joy bloom in her eyes when he spoke the words. "I'm glad because I love you."

The next week was a whirlwind as they prepared for their wedding. Paris had her furniture taken out of storage and delivered to Mac's house. Some of the cozy chintz pieces her mother had favored looked wildly out of place in the modern house, but they didn't care. Interior decorating wasn't on their minds very much.

They could only concentrate on each other and on the family they were creating for the children they loved and were determined to adopt. Elly was ecstatic about being a bridesmaid and having a dress that matched Becky's dress.

Paris would have happily married Mac wearing jeans and T-shirt, but Becky and June took her to Alban where she bought a simple floor-length blue sheath and matching veil. She carried a bouquet of roses because they'd been the favorite flowers of both her mother and Mac's.

She thought about the massive changes that had taken place in her life in the past and the hurts that had been healed.

"It's all worth it," she whispered to herself as she followed Elly and Becky from the house to the rock garden Mac had weeded so ruthlessly only a week before. The ocean crashed against the bottom of the cliff in an endless rhythm that gave her hope that their marriage would be as constant.

Paris loved this place. She was home now. She had wandered for a while, lost her way and found it again, and so had Mac. By some miracle, they had found each other.

Mac stood with the minister who was to perform the ceremony, and Grey, who was delighted to act as best man, especially if it meant being paired up with Becky. She had caught his interest and was the object of his good-natured teasing and flirting.

Elly and Simon clustered about Mac's feet and waited with him. Simon was content to listen to the music while he sucked his thumb and hugged a book to his new blue shirt, but Elly, annoyed at the slowness of "The

Wedding March,'' leaned forward, plopped her hands onto her hips, and whispered loudly. ''Hurry up, Pris. We're waiting.''

The small gathering of guests laughed, but when she reached Mac, he whispered. ''I've been waiting all my life.''

She covered his hand with hers and looked into his eyes. ''I'm here now. The wait's over. For both of us.''

He kissed her lightly on the cheek, echoed, ''For both of us,'' and turned with her to face the minister.

If you enjoyed what you just read,
then we've got an offer you can't resist!

Take 2 bestselling love stories FREE!

Plus get a FREE surprise gift!

Your Romantic Books—find them at

www.eHarlequin.com

Visit the *Author's Alcove*

➢ Find the most complete information anywhere on your favorite author.

➢ Try your hand in the Writing Round Robin— contribute a chapter to an online book in the making.

Enter the *Reading Room*

➢ Experience an interactive novel—help determine the fate of a story being created now by one of your favorite authors.

➢ Join one of our reading groups and discuss your favorite book.

Drop into *Shop eHarlequin*

➢ Find the latest releases—read an excerpt or write a review for this month's Harlequin top sellers.

➢ Try out our amazing search feature—tell us your favorite theme, setting or time period and we'll find a book that's perfect for you.

All this and more available at

www.eHarlequin.com
on Women.com Networks

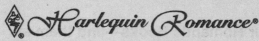